“Should we be worried?”

A loud clap of thunder rattled the windows, making several guests jump.

Reuben shook his head slightly. “Not yet. But if the time comes...” He hesitated, not wanting to frighten Nan but needing her to understand. “You’ll be safer with your family here. This farm is well situated and less likely to flood.”

Their eyes met, and something in her expression made his chest tighten. She didn’t dismiss his concern or laugh it off as others might have. Instead, she gave a slight nod, her blue eyes serious.

“I promise.” She spooned applesauce onto her plate, then added, “If you promise to actually stay for the singing.”

He opened his mouth to refuse, but she continued serving and passing the food as if she hadn’t just challenged him, as if she hadn’t noticed the way his breath caught at her request.

But when he glanced at Nan again, he caught the hint of a smile playing at her lips. She knew exactly how she affected him, and worse yet, he wasn’t entirely sure he minded.

Amy Grochowski's deep appreciation for the Amish faith and way of life stems from six years of living and working with a Beachy Amish family, as well as her own Anabaptist roots. After a nursing career of over twenty years, Amy is now fulfilling her long-awaited dream career as an author of inspirational romance. She is also a full-time homeschool mom for her two sons, one of whom has autism spectrum disorder. She lives with her family in the bustling foothills of North Carolina. Learn more at amygrochowski.com.

Books by Amy Grochowski

Love Inspired

The Amish Nanny's Promise
The Amish Baker's Secret Courtship
An Amish Love to Remember
A Secret Amish Arrangement

Visit the Author Profile page at LoveInspired.com.

A SECRET AMISH ARRANGEMENT

AMY GROCHOWSKI

Recycling programs for this product may not exist in your area.

ISBN-13: 978-1-335-62156-6

A Secret Amish Arrangement

For questions and comments about the quality of this book, please contact us at CustomerService@Harlequin.com.

Love Inspired
22 Adelaide St. West, 41st Floor
Toronto, Ontario M5H 4E3, Canada
www.LoveInspired.com

HarperCollins Publishers
Macken House, 39/40 Mayor Street Upper,
Dublin 1, D01 C9W8, Ireland
www.HarperCollins.com

Printed in Lithuania

I have blotted out, as a thick cloud,
thy transgressions, and, as a cloud, thy sins:
return unto me; for I have redeemed thee.
—*Isaiah* 44:22

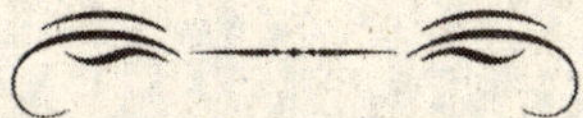

To David, who has traveled the path of recovery with faith, strength and grace beyond anything I ever might have dreamed. *Ich liebe dich*, for always.

Chapter One

All Nan Burkholder needed were a few fresh cuttings of Reuben Bender's lavender plants, but she couldn't find him to ask permission. He was *goot* at that—avoiding her. Standing on the highest hill of his lavender fields, Nan could see most everywhere except beyond the woods. Still no sight of him, only the sad remnants of his once vibrant purple rows of flowers, now charred and dying from a fire the previous summer.

The Amish had rallied to rebuild his barn. And not only members of their own mountain community here in Promise, Virginia, but nearly a hundred others from among the Amish and Mennonite congregations down in the valley had come, too. Almost a year had passed since then, but Reuben still hadn't returned to farming his lavender fields.

He might not have the heart to replant, but she wasn't ready to give up, not yet. Her supply of dried lavender was about to run out, especially as she'd be using a large quantity to brew her special tea for her sister's upcoming wedding. Lavender tea made from his locally grown harvest was her bestseller at Mattie's Amish Bakehouse in Promise and with her mail order customers too. She'd grow her own if she had to. All she needed were some healthy stems, and surely, among all the acres on this farm, a few plants had survived. There had to be enough to provide a dozen slips or so. And then, she could cultivate plants of her own in her *datt*'s small greenhouse.

Still locally grown. Still the same flavorful, aromatic variety her customers loved.

But first, she had to hunt down Reuben Bender.

Nan thrust her hands onto her hips and heaved a sigh, scanning the full-circle view of his Blue Ridge Mountains farm once more.

He had to be here somewhere. She'd been to the house first, and then the barn where his buggy, wagon and horses were all accounted for. Where was he?

A brisk summer breeze whipped strands of her blond hair from her *kapp*, plastering them against her face. She pulled a strand from her lips and gazed up at the sky. Without warning, dark clouds billowed across the mountain ridge from the west, eclipsing the sun.

Along the woods' edge, she noted the upturned leaves of the sweet gum and sycamore trees—a sure sign of a coming storm. She could dash back to the barn and take cover before the rain began. That was the sensible thing to do, she knew.

Nan hesitated a fraction of a heartbeat, between what she ought to do and what she'd come to do, then ran into the forest to search for Reuben.

She'd never been in this section of the woods before. On the other side to the northwest, her father owned a hunting lodge. The two properties met about halfway through the forested acres between them, but she'd never wandered too far beyond her *datt*'s cabin. And never had cause to traipse through Reuben's side, either.

Until now.

Her sister Rose likely knew all of this area by heart. Rose practically lived outdoors when she was younger. Nan wasn't too fond of the brambles sticking to her skirt. She daintily plucked a thorny vine from her dress, only to have another scratch against her arm.

"*Ach*, Reuben, but you are a nuisance," she muttered, not

caring that he couldn't hear her. "There better not be any poison ivy out here."

At least Rose had taught her how to identify the leaves of that horrible plant. Her eyes were peeled for any sign of it.

The patter of rain filtered down from the canopy of leaves above her until the first drop landed on her cheek. She swiped at it with the back of her hand. How long until the rain came harder and drenched her?

Nan crept deeper into the woods, hoping for a denser covering. Instead, she found herself among fewer and fewer trees. Rain pelted against her skin and clothing, just as an unexpected building came into her view.

Stunned at first, she stood gaping at a structure that appeared to be resurrected from old stone ruins. An enormous stone chimney, covered with lichen and moss, remained tall and formidable at one end, but the former stone walls of what must've once been a house centuries ago were mostly crumbled, slowly fallen away to nothing. She'd seen old, abandoned frontier homes reclaimed by the forest before.

But this was different. This one had been rebuilt. In place of the old stone walls, new heavy wooden beams of thick stained timbers stood strong and tight as a fortress with a roof of handhewn shingles. Three windows lined the horizontal length that stretched in front of her, the center one made of stained glass.

The whole of it was no larger than a one-room schoolhouse, but the sight was far more intriguing. The woodwork reminded her of Reuben's style. He'd made posts and signs and such for Amish businesses or *Englisch* customers who liked his work.

"For sure, this doesn't look Amish," she said aloud, wondering what possessed Reuben to rebuild such a structure. "I'm sure he hasn't told the bishop, either."

A smile ticked up the corners of her mouth at the thought of her *datt*, the bishop, and his opinion on that stained glass window. Well, she wouldn't be telling him about it.

The distant rumble of thunder moved her toward the only door on the end of the structure opposite the chimney. Thankful for the cover of a small awning above her, she pulled on the handle of the massive wooden door. It didn't even budge or rattle. But the large padlock hanging from the handle was open, leading her to believe someone was inside.

"Reuben!" She pounded on the door. "I know you're in there."

"Go away!" Reuben would know that voice anywhere, though he wished he didn't. "Mind your own business, Nan."

He winced. That came out harsher than he intended, but he was glad he'd locked the door from the inside this time. As persistent as Nan could be, she definitely couldn't push through that door. It weighed more than he did. And that was saying something.

He'd built a door and a frame even he couldn't knock down, and Reuben hadn't seen a man around taller or stronger than he was.

"*Bitte*, Reuben. It's raining."

Was it? He hadn't noticed. The sky had been clear when he came in here.

"What are you doing in my woods? In the rain? And how is that my problem?" He knew she wouldn't leave, though. Rain or not. Of course Nan, the bishop's youngest daughter, had to be the one to discover his haven from the world.

Reuben stood and put away the book he'd been reading, then glanced around to make sure nothing was left out to catch Nan's attention. She never missed a detail, that woman. Not a single one.

She was clever. He'd give her that.

He moved toward the door, attempting to be as quiet as possible so she wouldn't know he was about to capitulate. Now that she'd found him, she wouldn't give up.

"That's a lovely stained glass window, Reuben," she called sweetly through the door. *Ya*, Nan was clever. He understood the bribe hidden in the seemingly innocent statement.

But he didn't believe she'd tell the bishop. He couldn't say why exactly. Just that he didn't think that was Nan's way. She was nosy, persistent, smart and annoying. And beautiful. But she was more than that. She was also kindhearted and loyal.

Of course, she'd no reason to be loyal to him, he supposed, but he'd witnessed her devotion to her family and friends.

Lightning flashed just beyond the windows, illuminating the colored glass, immediately followed by a deafening crack of thunder.

At the threateningly close sound, Reuben wrenched the enormous door open and pulled Nan inside before slamming it shut against the weather.

"You're drenched." He was a terrible man. Had he really considered leaving her out there? Reuben looked her over, his guilt rising as he noticed the scratches on her arms. "And you're bleeding."

His hand lifted automatically toward the angry red lines on her skin, fingers almost brushing the worst of the scratches before he caught himself. He jerked back as if the almost-touch had burned him, shoving his hands into his pockets.

"Oh that. It's nothing. A wild rose of some sort." She rubbed her arm where his fingers had almost touched.

What was he thinking? Reuben rebuked himself for his momentary lapse of judgment. Nan was everything he'd tried to leave behind—curious, determined, unafraid to question. It was her fearlessness that troubled him the most—so like himself before his headstrong determination caused so much pain.

And now, she'd already skirted her way around him, her curious eyes taking in every aspect of his private sanctuary.

She turned slowly in a circle before coming back around to

face him. "It's a library." Her voice was a bare whisper. "You have built a library."

Her admiration tugged at the wall he'd only just erected to keep his feelings at bay. Seeing her appreciation for this place he loved felt like a bridge between them. Something they shared. But he couldn't afford a bridge between him and Nan—of all people.

"Not *a* library, Nan. *My* library. No one else knows. No one else has been inside. Not even Jake." He referred to his closest kin before closing the gap between them to stand in front of her. He looked down from the several inches he towered above her, even though she was tall. "And I'd like it to remain that way. Understand?"

She shuddered, though he hadn't intended to sound fierce. Besides, it would take a lot more than that to frighten Nan Burkholder.

"You're cold." The truth dawned on him. He moved to the fireplace, even if it was the middle of summer. She was wet, and the storm seemed to have dropped the temperature abruptly. Even in summer, he kept enough wood inside to heat a kettle of hot water, which should be enough to warm her and help her dry off.

He didn't even have two chairs. Didn't need more than one. So, he pulled his own up to the stove for her.

"Here, sit by the fire." He offered her the chair. He'd offer her anything at this point to keep her from rummaging around in his books and things.

Of all the people to find his library, why did it have to be the woman who could sniff out secrets like a hound after a squirrel?

Reuben sighed. Of course, Nan would find him, if anyone would.

But now, he had to make sure she didn't discover anything else.

"Why, Reuben?" Nan felt the soft chair he offered swallow her up like a cocoon. She could spend hours here by the stove or beneath that beautiful window with all of these books. Of course, he'd never allow it. "Why not share this with others?"

The stained glass might be a challenge to get approved, but surely *Datt* and the ministers would approve of a place of learning. The schoolchildren could benefit. And from the looks of some of the volumes, so could the farmers.

He hadn't answered her.

"Why keep all of this hidden?" *Other than his dislike for all but a select few people.* Nan bit her tongue to keep from answering for him.

She was definitely not on his list of likeable people. That short list included about four people: Reuben's cousin Jake and his fiancée, Aubrey, who happened to be Nan's oldest sister. Jake was raising two orphaned nephews, who both adored Reuben. And Reuben had a soft spot for both of the boys. Anyone could see that. He even seemed to be friendly toward Nan's best friend, Cassie, and her husband, Martin.

Alright, so that made six. Six people Reuben would speak to out of the entire Amish community here on Promise Mountain—that didn't make many. Their Blue Ridge Mountains town was remote. Promise, unincorporated, was a blink-of-an-eye town near the top of the mountain, and their Amish farms dotted the nearby hills and hollers of the surrounding miles. Maybe it seemed a great place for such a recluse, but their church family was exactly that—family. Blood related or not, they were a tight-knit community. Of course, many of them had lived here all their lives. But Reuben had moved to Promise almost five years ago and still kept to himself.

Perhaps it was mostly Nan that he took such pains to avoid. She'd sometimes wondered, but this place stood as evidence that he truly didn't want to be around anyone else much.

She glanced around the winged back of the leather upholstered armchair where she was sitting. Reuben was pacing, his hands behind his back, going from window to window, presumably waiting for the storm to pass so he could send her on her way again.

He still hadn't answered her question, unless he thought a growl counted.

And it certainly didn't satisfy her.

She stood and wandered toward a large table between them. Books were stacked on it, five, ten, twelve deep in places. Underneath a pile close to her, some loose papers jutted out at odd angles. Even from where she stood, she could see the elegant loops of handwriting—bearing the distinctive quality of a bygone generation—on the exposed corner.

She looked up to find Reuben. He stood with his back to her, staring out the window, but Reuben's shoulders tensed, and his hands gripped so tightly that his knuckles whitened. He knew exactly where she was. And he didn't like it.

But Nan had never been good at backing away from mysteries.

She reached out to straighten the papers, telling herself she was just tidying, even as her heart quickened with curiosity about what secrets that aged writing might reveal.

"Don't." Reuben was on the opposite side of the table from her in one long stride. His hand came down on the pile of books, sliding the papers completely out of sight in one swift movement. His voice was soft but carried an edge she'd never heard before. "I mean it, Nan."

Most women would jump at that gravelly, authoritative voice of his, even though he'd spoken as softly as she'd ever heard him. But Nan merely removed her hand slowly.

Most women would apologize. But Nan refused. What had she done wrong?

Nothing.

He was the one hiding more than a library. But Nan had known for a long time that Reuben had secrets. She'd already apologized for spreading rumors when he first came to Promise. And she hadn't gossiped about his past again.

In fact, she hadn't meddled in his business, or tried to discover why he'd moved to this mountain all alone, ever again. Not even once. Which was no small feat for a curious mind. And she hadn't come looking for this library of his, either.

She'd stumbled upon it while on a mission for her own business. And he let her in.

Still, the man deserved his privacy.

As hard as it was to let go of the threads of a secret right in front of her, Nan looked steadily up into Reuben's amber brown eyes and raised her chin. "I came to ask you if I could gather some slips of lavender. I'd like to grow some in *Datt*'s greenhouse to make tea."

"Lavender." For a heartbeat, he looked confused, then straightened to his full height. "You came to me for lavender?"

"*Ya*, Reuben, lavender. You know, the acres of plants you've neglected since the fire. Since you haven't replanted yet, and a harvest from seed will take at least two more seasons, I'd like to grow some of my own. I'm sure I can find some undamaged plants out there and salvage enough for my purposes."

Understanding seemed to dawn, mixed with some surprise, on his face. He turned away from her to look out the window once more.

"The rain seems to have stopped. If lavender is what you want—" He strode to the giant door at the end of the room and opened the door wide, then swirled around to face her and waved an arm toward the outdoors. "Be my guest."

She wasn't surprised in the least that Reuben was glad to be rid of her or that the summer squall had gone as fast as it had come. But she made the mistake of looking over her shoulder before he closed the door behind her. He was watching her, his shoulders slumped.

She shouldn't have looked back. Shouldn't have let his lonely, if giant, figure tug at her heart. But it was too late.

When his gaze met hers, she asked, "You'll be at the wedding, won't you?"

"You think I'd let my cousin down?" Offense laced his tone. "I'll be there as Jake's side-sitter, same as you'll be there with your sister."

"I didn't mean it like that." She hadn't meant to insinuate he'd leave Jake short a groomsman, no matter how he detested festive gatherings. The bride and groom each had two *Newesitzer*, attendants who sat beside them both during the church ceremony and afterward at the head table for luncheon. "I knew you'd show up for church and even for the meal following. I meant later…for the supper and singing. You aren't usually at those kinds of social things. But I thought maybe for Jake… So, will you be staying?"

"Why would you want to know that?" He stepped out of the door, forcing her to take a step backward.

Because of who she might be paired up with for the special meal. She didn't have a date, but someone—a single young man—would be chosen to sit with her, and she dreaded it. "I just thought… I don't like that tradition of being paired up. People think things. And there's no one I want thinking of me in that way."

"People do think things, don't they, Nan?" His mouth curved into the closest thing to a smile she'd seen since he'd opened the door and yanked her inside from the storm.

"Tease me all you want. I know I have a reputation for being a gossip."

He frowned. "That is not what I meant. I forgave you for that long ago. I haven't ever brought it up, have I." It wasn't a question, but Nan shook her head, anyway.

"*Nay*, you haven't." Of course, he hadn't brought up much of anything with her, ever. But she saw his point, now that he mentioned it. Reuben had truly forgiven her. "Well, then, what did you mean?"

The sun came out, shining between the trees and reflecting the auburn highlights in his otherwise dark beard. He'd never been married, yet he kept a beard.

"I meant that if you are trying to get around to asking me to stay and sit with you at the marriage feast, I will. Is that what you were hoping for, Nan? For me to scare off any unwanted suitors?"

Her answer caught in her throat. She hadn't exactly meant to ask him that. Had she? But the memory of John Beachy's father cornering *Datt* at the last wedding, of the expectations in everyone's eyes—as if having fun with John at a wedding was akin to a plea for a proposal and a scandal to refuse it—made her stomach clench.

"I don't have any suitors." More like tormentors, in her opinion. "But *ya*, I would appreciate it." Not that Reuben was particularly scary, not to her, especially now that she'd seen his library. A man who read…well, she felt she'd seen another side of Reuben Bender this morning. Besides, his reputation for keeping people at a distance would work in her favor.

"And people will talk." One of his thick dark brows lifted. "What then?"

Nan hadn't had a chance to think that far. She straightened her spine, as if they were questioning her already. "Better they whisper about me and you than having to endure another round of matchmaking. Last time…"

She stopped herself. No need to mention how adamantly she'd defended herself against being pushed into a relationship, especially with John Beachy. Or anyone, for that matter, who declared himself willing to overlook her many faults because she was so pretty. Her *datt* had barely managed to smooth things over when the Beachys threatened trouble after the tongue-lashing she'd given John.

"Last time?" There was something knowing in Reuben's voice.

"It doesn't matter." She didn't like thinking that he probably knew all about her humiliation. "We go on as usual, I suppose. You continue to ignore me, and I… I continue to avoid the matchmakers."

He looked down at her as if assessing whether she had some other trick up her sleeve. As if he, too, was weighing the cost of such an arrangement.

"That's all. Truly." She put a hand on her hip. "Wait. Are you actually considering doing this for me? I have to say, I'm a little surprised you haven't said no already."

He laughed. Sort of. She hadn't heard Reuben laugh before and couldn't be quite sure whether the sound he quickly cut short was a chuckle or a groan. "Maybe because I understand what it's like to have others meddle in your future. Or question your faith because you don't always fit their idea of what being *goot* Amish means."

Nan sucked in a sharp breath. Wasn't that exactly what John had said, that she was pretty enough to overlook her un-Amish habits? She felt her cheeks grow hot at the memory. How dare he? Because she told him no, he felt justified in questioning her devotion to her faith.

Reuben stepped closer, his amber eyes warm with compassion. "Maybe because you considered asking me, rather than letting your sister make an arrangement for you." His voice deepened. "Or perhaps because I know exactly how persistent folks like Dan and John Beachy can be."

That last comment made her catch her breath. What did he know? All the past few years of trying to stay out of Reuben's business. Of ignoring the mystery of his past. All her virtuous attempts to respect his privacy seemed to crumble.

"What do you know about the Beachys?" She stepped closer

to him, gauging the battled expression on his face. And for one brief second, she thought he might open up to her.

"Don't push it, Nan. I will be your supper partner, and I'll escort you safely home after the singing. John Beachy won't ruin your sister's special day for you." He peered down at her. "But keep my library and its whereabouts to yourself. This is my private library, and I intend to keep it that way." His height towered over hers, but she didn't shrink back. "Do we have a deal?"

"Fine, I shouldn't have pushed for more about the Beachys." But he didn't need to know that she never even considered telling a soul about his secret place. Though she had hoped to use her knowledge to bargain for access to it for herself. "It's a deal, and I thank you for it, too."

Reuben nodded, and the tense strain of his jaw relaxed, though the gruffness in his voice remained. "But Nan? Don't mistake this for anything more than a convenient arrangement for Jake and Aubrey's wedding. I have my reasons for avoiding social gatherings. One wedding supper won't change that. Don't go getting the idea you can reform my ways."

He spun away, then called over his shoulder from the doorway of his library. "Take all the lavender you want, if you can find any. I plan to till it all up and have no plans to plant more ever again."

"Reuben. You can't be serious."

"I am. Perfectly."

He pushed the heavy door shut. *And don't come back*, the click of the lock seemed to say.

It wasn't much of a deal they'd struck, in her opinion. But when had an encounter with Reuben left her anything but disappointed?

He always hid behind a mysterious cloak of sadness, even more so since the fire last summer.

But she'd have her lavender. She'd be free from any attempts by John to escort her to supper and the singing. And no one would be pestering her sister to seat her with a nephew or a cousin or a brother-in-law who needed a partner for the wedding. And for sure and certain, Reuben wouldn't mistake anything she said or did as flirting or looking for a marriage proposal. But perhaps he'd have a *goot* time, in spite of himself. *Ach*, wouldn't she like to see that?

And then after this, nothing would change, which was for the best.

Except for the fact that now she knew Reuben Bender had a magnificent library hidden in his woods. She'd keep his secret, but she hadn't made any deals or promises about not coming back again. A good thing, too, since she'd dearly love to visit that library—and often.

Reuben wouldn't like it, of course.

And that sounded like a challenge she couldn't pass up.

Chapter Two

Reuben scanned the volumes on his shelves, searching for his collection of farmer's almanacs. He'd found the *Raber's Amish Almanac* that he was looking for. His collection of those dated all the way back to the first printing in 1930. But he was hunting for two particular years of the *Englischer*'s almanac, 1969 and 1985, hoping for more specific information regarding the Southern Appalachian Mountains region. That collection wasn't as complete, and he feared he didn't have what he was looking for.

Either that or his brain remained addled from Nan's visit last week. He'd surprised himself, potentially even more than he'd shocked Nan, when he offered to sit with her at the wedding supper. He'd heard about the incident with John Beachy. The whole thing had irritated him at the time, but then realizing that Nan was still troubled by it had riled his protective nature.

He had no patience for men like Dan and John Beachy. He was well acquainted with a few of their relatives in Lancaster, and Nan's experience proved these cousins of theirs in Promise were of the same ilk—bound to get their way with a heavy hand and plow anyone under who stood in their way.

Nan deserved credit for standing up to them, not ridicule. And he wasn't too proud to admit, at least to himself, that he respected her for it.

Nay, something else—something he couldn't put a finger on—had him *verhuddelt* since her visit, or visits to be more accurate. She hadn't returned to the library, but she'd been to the farm at least twice more searching for living lavender plants. He could have told her it was a useless endeavor, but he'd stayed out of sight, leaving her and her wishful notions alone.

Taking a closer look at the section of his library shelves filled with farming manuals, nature guides and historical weather accounts, he finally found exactly what he was searching for—a misplaced stapled booklet, too thin for regular binding. 1985. *Wunderbar.*

Now to find the other. He ran an index finger along the shelf. *"Vo bist du?"* Where are you?

There. Behind his grandfather's old leather-bound dairy ledger. Reuben pulled out another thin booklet, this one's cover worn and water stained. 1969. The year his *datt* and *grossdawdi* had nearly lost everything to flooding in Lancaster County.

Settling into his chair, he opened both almanacs side by side. The similarities in the weather patterns leading up to both disasters were unmistakable. High rainfall in early spring. Then a dry spell. Then unusual humidity and high temperatures in August, followed by…

His hands trembled slightly as he lifted his own weather journal from the desk. He'd been recording patterns since arriving in Promise, just as his *dawdi* had taught his *datt*, and his *datt* had taught him. The entries from the past month matched the old records with frightening accuracy.

"Helfe uns Gott." Help us. The plea for *Gott*'s wisdom and protection escaped in a whisper.

He stood abruptly, gathering the almanacs and his journal. The bishop needed to see this. Pride had cost him everything once before. He wouldn't let it cost others now.

Reuben carefully returned the leather ledger to its shelf, his fingers lingering on its spine. Three generations of careful observations were recorded in that book. His *dawdi*'s neat columns of figures, his *datt*'s precise notes, then his own—ending abruptly the year everything fell apart.

When it all came to an end on Reuben's watch.

He tucked the almanacs and journal into his coat. What he must do was bound to bring his past right back to the tips of wagging tongues, especially as he was already bound to upset Dan and John Beachy by sitting with Nan.

"Vas muss sein, muss sein." What must be, must be.

Reuben had no pride left now, anyway. The bishop would want proof of what he was about to tell him. And maybe, just maybe, helping prevent disaster here could begin to make up for what he couldn't prevent before.

Nan couldn't help but smile at the tiny white roots emerging from the lavender cuttings. After only a week, they were already reaching for life in her *datt*'s greenhouse. She touched one of the tender shoots gently, hardly daring to believe how many had survived.

She'd found far more healthy plants among Reuben's burned fields than she'd expected. Each of the ten nursery trays contained fifty small cells, and in every cell, a lavender slip stretched its leaves toward the glass ceiling. Five hundred plants in all. She'd gone back to his farm three times to harvest so many, motivated by the notion she might change Reuben's mind. If all these slips survived and grew into plants, she'd have enough for a half acre.

"Not so much compared to what Reuben had before, but far more than I could ever use for selling my teas, even if business at the bakery doubled." She spoke aloud to the tender shoots, as she often did when alone. The lavender didn't seem to mind her chatter. "And hopefully enough to show him it's worth trying again."

The thought of Reuben giving up on his lavender fields bothered her. Before the fire, those purple rows had been the pride of Promise Mountain. Even the *Englisch* tourists would stop to take pictures when they drove past.

A clatter from outside drew her attention. Through the greenhouse glass, she saw Reuben's distinctive black wagon parked near her *datt*'s forge. Her heart did an odd little skip. Reuben could be here for any number of reasons, from blacksmithing needs to business with the bishop. A horse that needed shoeing or wedding details to discuss with her *datt*, since Reuben was cousin to the groom and her *datt* was father of the bride.

But ever since he'd agreed to sit with her at the wedding supper, she'd had an uneasy feeling that something unexpected was coming. Like the stillness before a storm.

She pulled off her gardening apron and smoothed her dress. No sense in looking like she'd been crawling around in the dirt if she was going to investigate his visit. Not that Reuben would notice or care what she looked like. Still.

The humid air hit her as soon as she stepped outside. Even the weather felt strange lately, heavy with secret plans. Or she could be imagining things. She'd been doing that more often since finding Reuben's library.

Voices drifted from the forge—her *datt*'s steady tone and Reuben's deeper rumble. She moved closer, telling herself she wasn't really eavesdropping. After all, she had every right to be curious about a visitor to her own home.

"—unusual weather for August," she heard her *datt* say. "The spring's running higher than I've ever seen it this time of year. Higher even than before the flood of '85."

"That's even more confirmation, don't you agree?" Reuben's voice carried an edge of something… Worry? "The patterns remind me of—"

He cut off abruptly. Nan realized too late that her shadow had fallen across the entrance to the forge.

"Nan." Her *datt*'s face creased with a smile above his long white beard. "Come home early to check on your plants again?"

Her father's question only partially registered. She was watching Reuben and wondering why his shoulders had tensed at her arrival. Whatever he'd been about to say to *Datt*, he wouldn't continue now.

"*Ya*, I did all I could to help Aubrey and Rose for today." Their grandmother's sunflower farm was going to be beautiful for the wedding. And the renovations Jake had completed on the log cabin made a perfect home for Aubrey, Jake and the two boys. "Tomorrow morning, I can bake the bread at Cassie's bakery when I go to work. She's already planning to help me."

"And how are your lavender plants coming along?" her *datt* prodded again.

"*Ach*, sorry, *Datt*. I was distracted by…the wedding plans." That was a truthful enough reason. Still, she knew her father saw straight through her to the real distraction, evidenced by the way his brow lifted and his eyes darted to Reuben, then back at her.

She stepped into the forge, pretending not to notice how Reuben edged away from her. "The cuttings are doing well. All *five hundred* of them. Seems your plants were more resilient than you gave them credit for, particularly the ones in the field near Martin's beehives."

Reuben's jaw sagged open, and his eyes lingered on her face a moment too long before he looked away.

"Five hundred," he repeated, recovering nicely from his surprise. But something in his voice made her wonder if he was more impressed by the number or by her determination. "You'll have plenty for your tea business, then."

"More than enough, actually." She met his gaze steadily. "Enough to share, if someone wanted to replant their fields. Enough for a small harvest next year to bridge the gap between those and a seed crop."

Her father's eyes moved between them, but he said nothing.

And neither did Reuben, though his gaze held hers intently, as if to drive home the message that he hadn't changed his mind.

After a long moment, Reuben turned back to her *datt*.

"We'll finish our discussion later, Bishop Naaman." He reached for his hat. "About the other matter."

"Of course." Her *datt*'s voice was gentle, the same tone he used when counseling troubled members of their community. "But consider what I said. Some burdens aren't meant to be carried alone."

Reuben's only response was a curt nod as he strode past Nan. She caught a whiff of sawdust from his workshop. Maybe even the scent of old books followed him. But there was something else, too—worry rolled off him in almost visible waves.

"What was that about?" she asked her *datt* once Reuben was out of earshot.

"He's worried about the weather." *Datt* shrugged. "Though not without cause. We've had more rain than usual."

"The weather?" Reuben sure was behaving more mysteriously than a man worried about some rain. "I believe he's bothered by something more than that."

Her *datt* picked up a horseshoe, studying it with unnecessary attention. "*Vell*, since you'll be sitting with him at the wedding supper, perhaps you'll have a chance to speak with him yourself. Although, you'd be wise not to press him too far. I may have advised him to let others help carry his burdens, but that choice is his to make. You cannot force him."

"*Nay*, *Datt*, I wouldn't try." She recognized the unbelieving twinkle in her father's eye at that. "I didn't coerce him into sitting with me at the wedding supper, if that's what you're thinking. We made an arrangement, that's all. To avoid…complications."

"Did you now?" He set down the horseshoe. "And does this arrangement explain why Reuben Bender, who hasn't voluntarily spoken to you in years, is suddenly concerned about your safety in bad weather?"

"*My* safety?" The uneasy feeling in her stomach grew. "What do you mean?"

But her *datt* just smiled and turned back to his work, humming an old hymn as if he hadn't just dropped a puzzle in her lap.

Nan looked toward the wagon now disappearing down the lane. First the library, then the wedding arrangement, and now this cryptic visit about weather patterns.

If Reuben wanted her to leave him alone, he sure was going about it all wrong. If she'd been curious before, it was nothing compared to her level of interest now. The itch to figure him out was worse than the poison ivy rash she'd gotten on her ankles despite her best efforts to avoid the horrible stuff in his woods.

What are you up to, Reuben?

Whatever it was suddenly felt as if it was very much her business. And this time she wasn't just being nosy.

Aubrey and Jake's wedding was only two short days away. Her *datt* was right—she'd have more of an opportunity to speak with Reuben than ever before. And she planned to make the most of it.

Something told her this mystery might matter more than any secret she'd ever uncovered.

Chapter Three

Reuben hadn't come to regret his deal with Nan, not yet. But this day was in its early stages. Things could change. Fast. How well he knew it, as he sat in the barn on the Burkholders' sunflower farm for the wedding of his cousin Jake to the bishop's oldest daughter, Aubrey.

Amish marriage ceremonies never changed, however. As far as he knew, they were the one definite custom that didn't vary from district to district. Some wedding traditions and preferences in the activities that followed might differ from one church to another, but the worship service ritual was always the same.

As long as the three hours could be, Reuben found some comfort in knowing exactly what to expect. Though his body did ache from sitting up straight for so long on a backless wooden bench. One couldn't exactly slouch this close to front and center.

Nan was seated directly in front of him, wearing a bright blue dress that matched her eyes, and beside each of them were the empty chairs left by the bride and groom as they'd exited with the ministers. The congregation sang, waiting for their return from the traditional twenty-minute or so counseling session. Then, during another sermon, their vows would be spoken. In all, he expected there was another hour left until everyone was dismissed for the luncheon to follow.

Sixty more minutes of eye contact with Nan. And the avoidance of it.

He wasn't the only person she had her eyes on, either. And he'd made a diverting game out of guessing who she was watching behind him and what she was thinking in that observant mind of hers.

Being so near to her, he'd made a discovery of his own. Nan Burkholder possessed a lovely singing voice. Somehow, he'd never known it before now. He found himself straining forward to get closer to her each time a hymn was sung.

She noticed.

Of course, she did.

She was looking straight at him and had stopped singing the words, though her lips continued to move. Between the movements of her mouth and her expression, he caught her silent reprimand. *You're not singing.*

He replied by making a show of mouthing the words of the song, without using his voice. He was a terrible singer. For sure and certain, he didn't want her to know, not now that he'd heard her sing.

She rolled her eyes at him and continued to sing, while he continued to pretend.

As the song came to an end, a reverent hush fell over the entire congregation. The ministers entered the barn, along with Jake and Aubrey, walking down the center aisle between the men's and women's sides. Every soul in the room watched as the bride and groom took their respective places for the coming marriage vows.

But before that most sacred moment, the congregation sang another hymn, and Reuben focused on the soothing tones of Nan's voice throughout the singing until her father began the final sermon of the morning. The sweet sound of her voice eased something in his soul that had been tight and painful for so long, he'd forgotten what peace felt like.

Finally, the last amen was pronounced. A moment not lost on anyone as the bride and groom beamed at one another.

As the wedding party stood to make their exit, Reuben leaned close to his cousin and thumped him on the back. "Congratulations, Jake. May all your days be as happy as this one."

Jake's grin grew a little wider, though Reuben wasn't sure how that was possible, as they all filed into the Burkholders' old family farmhouse where Nan and Aubrey's grandmother lived.

In short order, they were seated at the *Eck*—two long tables placed together at the head of the largest room, forming an L-shape in a corner where the wedding party could sit facing the rest of the room. Another long-standing tradition he knew to expect.

Reuben was seated with the groom on one side and Jake's other attendant, Lukas, at the other. Nan sat between her two sisters at the adjoining side of the *Eck*, while the room filled up with unmarried *youngies*, guys on one side of the row of tables and the gals opposite them, just beginning to loosen up to enjoy the day's coming activities.

The chatter of the crush was jarring after the solemnity of the worship service. His foot tapped under the table, thankfully hidden by the tablecloth.

He looked down at the setting of wedding china in front of him. He should say something. Compliment Jake on his choice of a sunflower pattern—a gift from the groom to the bride—that matched the rest of the yellow and sunburned orange decorations. An appropriate choice for the couple who would be running the family sunflower farm together.

He opened his mouth, then shut it.

He'd have to yell over the growing noise. And how *schtupid* would he sound shouting about dinner plate patterns? Ridiculous.

Nan had guessed correctly. He would much prefer to leave as soon as this meal ended, rather than remain for all the shenanigans to come. And that wretched supper with all the matchmaking nonsense.

Because who was he kidding? Nan could fend for herself. She didn't really need his help. The only thing worth all this socializing was maintaining the privacy of his library. And he didn't really think she'd tell anyone about his library, even if he did back out of his end of their deal. Ever since her apology for spreading rumors about him, she'd respected his privacy. He'd noticed, and his estimation of her had risen from then on.

Regardless, he wouldn't leave. He'd given her his word. And now, he'd see this thing through.

Reuben leaned his chair back for a view around the bride and groom to see Nan. At least he'd have the comfort of her singing, he was thinking when she caught him looking.

"What?" she mouthed.

He shrugged and tapped his wind-up wristwatch, as if to say this was taking forever.

"Too bad." At least that's what he thought she'd mimed back to him.

He sat forward again to face the room full of people. The scent of roast beef drifted by him, making his stomach rumble.

The food would be *goot*. There was that. And there was another upside to staying. Every bishop in the valley was here today. And if he wanted to warn them about his concerns, this was the perfect time.

Martin and Cassie Beiler approached the head table, both carrying water and tea pitchers. They were one of the young married couples chosen to serve for the wedding. Cassie was Nan's best friend and owned the local bakery. She seemed right in her element, as happy in a crowd as Nan.

Martin, however, might be the one person as miserable as Reuben. He was valiantly doing his duty, though.

"Tea or water?" he asked Reuben.

"Sweet tea, *denki*." Reuben finally found something worth

saying. "I was wondering, Martin, how did your beehives on my farm fare this summer? You know, without the lavender, since the fire. I feared they might not do well."

Appearing happy to talk about a subject he loved, Martin set the pitchers down. "*Nay*, turns out my bees and your lavender worked things out. The bees found enough pollen to fill the hives with honey. Might not be as strong a lavender flavor as past seasons. I suspect they foraged elsewhere for more nectar, but they managed."

Interesting. "Well, I may owe you some thanks. It appears your bees helped the area closest to them recover better than the rest of my fields. Quite honestly, I hadn't held out any hope for that." Wouldn't have noticed, either, if not for Nan.

Martin smiled and picked his drink pitchers back up, realizing Cassie had already moved down the other tables. "Thank *Gott* for that. His creation is remarkable."

And sometimes fierce. But Reuben kept his worries about what nature might have in store to himself, at least for the time being. However, as soon as the meal was over, he had some bishops and church elders to seek out.

"Do you regret our deal yet?" Nan found Reuben lingering at the outside edges of an impromptu volleyball game late in the afternoon. "Seems you've found plenty to talk about to nearly every bishop in the state of Virginia."

He grunted, but she saw the corner of his mouth tick upward. "You exaggerate."

"Not by much." She lingered by his side, noticing he was somehow more at ease with her since her visit to his library. Or was she the one more comfortable with him?

"I should've known you'd notice." He didn't sound annoyed, just stating a fact. "Happens to be *goot* timing to discuss concerns with them, having so many all gathered at once."

"Don't think I haven't noticed you are worried about something, Reuben. Can't you talk to me about it?"

He pivoted to look directly down at her. The amber of his eyes caught the afternoon sun as it broke through a cloud above them. "Flooding, Nan. Not to be an alarmist, mind you. I have reason to be concerned about what a heavy rain, or worse, high winds and heavy rains, could do with the ground already saturated."

"You mean that hurricane headed toward Florida?" She couldn't figure why he was so concerned about a storm so far away. "I haven't heard any weather reports about it coming close to us. And I have been listening out for weeks because of the wedding. We'd have had to do things very differently if it rained today." She glanced up at the partially cloudy sky. "Seems we dodged it, if barely. I think we might get rain tomorrow."

"I'm not a weatherman. Or a prophet, Nan. And it is a blessing that the weather has been cooperative today. But it is still hurricane season, and our streams are all running high already."

"We don't get hurricanes in the mountains, Reuben."

"Pray we don't, Nan."

His serious tone was chilling, though she still didn't understand it. Sure, they got the big storms' leftovers sometimes, but they dealt with that kind of thing nearly every year.

She remembered what *Datt* had said about Reuben being worried for her safety. Probably not so much about her, specifically, but for everyone, she supposed. And perhaps in his glum frame of mind, still oppressed from the devastation of the wildfire, Reuben was overreacting. And yet, he was thinking of others, and for that, she respected his concerns.

"I will pray." Without forethought, she gently touched her fingertips to his shoulder. To her surprise, the action felt natural, and he didn't shake her off. Instead, he looked reassuringly back at her as her hand fell away.

"Don't you two look cozy?" She recognized John Beachy's

nasal tone without turning to see him before he came around from behind. "I wouldn't put too much stock into it, if I were you, Reuben. Nan will lead any man on. Just won't follow through when it gets serious."

A menacing growl rumbled from deep within Reuben's chest, and John backed off.

"Don't say I didn't warn you." John held up a defensive hand, then turned away, disappearing faster than he'd snuck up on them.

"*Denki*, Reuben."

"For what?" His hands were gripped by his sides. He slowly released them and exhaled deeply. "Not punching him?"

Laughter burst from her, and she couldn't stop it. He'd been holding his temper with John, for sure, but he'd been controlling his tongue as much as anything. Still, he'd managed to scare John off with nothing but a stare and a growl. His ironic response tickled her and eased the stress of the moment. "He'd have had to turn the other cheek, if you did."

Reuben shook his head at her, as if she had been very naughty to say such a thing, but all the tension in his posture had relaxed. "The things you say, Nan."

"You started it."

He smiled, which gave her an unexpected sense of satisfaction.

He was caring and considerate under his aloof demeanor. He might actually have a sense of humor, too. Wonders never ceased. She felt guilty, then, for making a deal that would only make him miserable the rest of the evening.

"I'll be okay." She glanced up at him, and he was staring at her. Question lines furrowed his brow. "I mean, you don't have to stay. I know you don't really want to."

"You know that, do you?" Something in his gaze made her question what she knew to be true. But he'd already told her not to try to change him. She couldn't quite decipher the look he was sending her, because he wouldn't have changed his mind. Would he?

"I won't tell about the library, if you want to leave. And I won't need a ride back to mine and *Datt*'s house. I can stay here at *grossmammi*'s tonight. They need me to help clean up all of this in the morning, anyway. I'd just have to come back. I didn't say so earlier because..." Because it had been so thoughtful of him to offer her a ride. Because it had seemed genuinely romantic. Because he must be messing with her mind. "Because..."

"Fine, Nan, I don't require any further excuses. I get the point. I'll go, since that's obviously what you want." His gruff demeanor had returned. "I doubt John will bother you again, but I will stay through the supper. I intend to at least keep my end of the bargain. Then I will leave you alone to enjoy yourself for the singing."

She sucked in a breath. Suddenly, she realized that she'd made a terrible mistake. "Reuben, I'm sorry. I thought—"

"Don't explain, Nan. It's not necessary." He was already walking away.

What had she done? This wasn't what she wanted at all.

Through the crowd, she caught sight of John's father, Dan Beachy, speaking intently with one of the visiting bishops, both men glancing frequently toward Reuben's retreating figure. The older man's face grew grave as Dan spoke, and Nan's stomach clenched.

All these bishops in one place might've been beneficial to Reuben for sharing his concerns about the rising waters, but it was also helpful to anyone trying to start trouble.

Whatever secrets Reuben was trying to protect, she had a feeling they wouldn't stay hidden much longer.

Chapter Four

Nan worked her way through the wedding crowd and found her sister Aubrey leaning against the large oak tree waiting for her. The sky was a touch too dark for late afternoon, thanks to increasing cloud cover.

"Looks like a rain that's going to settle in for a while," Nan noted as she handed Aubrey her wedding planner.

"But thankfully not too soon. I think it'll stay dry for supper, at least, and probably for the singing afterward, too. Doesn't feel like rain yet." Aubrey accepted the notebook with the guest names, scowling down at the long list of unmarried youngies. "I'm too old for this. I wish you could do this for me."

"You're only thirty-one. And it's *your* wedding day, Aubrey. The supper seating arrangement is the bride's task."

"*Ya*, Nan, I know. I'm perfectly happy with the wedding… and my age. I rather think it might be better to marry with a little more maturity. And for sure and certain, I am blessed to have found love with Jake. It's all of *this* that stresses me out."

Aubrey tapped the papers open in front of her. "I know some brides adore making all these matches, but to me it feels a little like…playing *Gott*. And besides, you know more about all these *kinner* and their likes and dislikes and probably even their crushes. Just whisper what you think to me."

Nan chose to overlook her sister's reference to the youth as *kinner*. Some were as young as sixteen, quite eager, nervous and likely being set up for the first time in their lives. But Nan was almost twenty-two and in no way a child. And Reuben?

"How old is Reuben, anyway?" she asked Aubrey.

"I believe he's a couple years younger than Jake and me. Twenty-eight or nine, maybe. Why? You already asked to be seated with him. He's not ancient or anything."

Nan shrugged. "Just wondering. Can you believe I didn't know?"

"Well, there's a first for everything." Aubrey laughed. "So, stay and help me, will you?"

As if Nan could resist. Though she'd have to be discreet.

Folks were already whispering about her and Reuben. It would be much better if they assumed the pairing had been Aubrey's idea and not her own.

Reuben wouldn't like being paired up with her permanently in people's minds. This was a onetime deal, as he'd made very clear.

Funny, though, he hadn't told her not to get any romantic ideas, just no ideas about reforming him. How had he pegged her so well? Because right now, she wished he would be at events like this more often, despite their misunderstanding earlier. And she just might consider trying to change his reclusive ways a bit.

"So, what is going on with you and Reuben?" Aubrey's voice was barely a whisper. "He seems different today."

"*Ya*, he does." Or he did, up until she gave him the impression she didn't want him to stay. "But it won't last. He's only humoring me because..."

Aubrey's brow rose at her near slip. "Because?"

Nan pretended not to hear and began rattling off some names for the seating arrangement instead. Pairing up supper partners was far easier than figuring out Reuben Bender.

"You're hiding something, *schwester*, but then so is Reuben." Aubrey tsked her tongue. "Sounds like a dangerous match."

She held her pen above Nan and Reuben's names, as if she'd mark them off.

"You won't do it."

"So, you really do want this arrangement?" Aubrey withdrew her pen. "I wonder what I will find happening with you two when we return from our wedding trip?"

"Nothing. I can assure you." Nan huffed and swiped the notebook from her sister. So much for being discreet. At this rate, they'd be having supper at midnight unless she took charge. "Now, let me think."

"Go ahead." Aubrey grinned, having gotten her way.

Not that Nan minded. She was perfectly happy to play as a matchmaker. She just didn't want to be matched. She zipped down the list, pairing off almost everyone with ease. But then, there was an extra name, and no *maidel* left to pair with him.

"We have one too many guys." Nan tapped the pen over John Beachy's name. No surprise he was the lone straggler. Nan didn't wish him on any girl. "What am I supposed to do with him?"

"He asked to be seated with you." Aubrey sounded much too happy to reveal this tidbit that made Nan squirm.

"What? Why would he do that?" She'd been nervous about who she might have to sit with but hadn't expected John to try again.

"I suppose to find out if the rumors are true that Reuben will be your partner. And it's no secret. I mean, in another hour everyone will know."

"So, what did you say?"

"I told him I had other requests, so I'd have to see what could be done. And Nan, I don't think it wise to leave him as the only one without a partner. He won't take it kindly."

"Well, I can't pull another girl out of thin air." Nan pushed her hands onto her hips. "Someone has to be left without a partner. What do you suggest?"

"You can add Rose to the list." Aubrey put a finger to her lips before Nan could object to involving their middle sister. "I know she prefers not to participate, but she offered if necessary. And *nay*, I don't mean to put her with John. She can sit with Lukas. Jake's cousin has been very kind to her since he arrived for the wedding a few days ago. And that frees up one more person to sit with John. Surely, he's not that bad. There must be a girl on that list who could appreciate his company."

"If you say so..." Nan didn't bother hiding her disbelief that such a girl existed. But Rose was painfully shy. Nan could hardly believe Aubrey would make her participate, even if it did solve the seating problem. "But must we sacrifice poor Rose?"

"*Ach*, you're being silly. Lukas is a *goot* man, Nan. And Rose agreed she would do it if needed."

Nan didn't like it, but this wasn't her wedding or her call. "I'll go let her know, if you like? Give her a few minutes to get her nerve up."

"It's just a meal, Nan, in the house where she lives. She'll be *oll recht*. I think she'd be much better off if everyone stopped hovering over her so much."

"I'm not sure about that." Rose had always seemed fragile to Nan. "But then I don't know her like you do." Not only was there a big age gap with her sisters, but since their *mamm* had died, Nan had lived with their *datt*, while Aubrey and Rose lived with their *grossmammi*. "And I was too young to understand everything that was happening or what made her so shy."

"She was always shy, even before *Mamm* died. But she's not helpless or weak as everyone seems to suppose." Aubrey let out a concerned sigh. "I'll decide who to pair with John and make the necessary adjustments."

Nan knew when to concede to her oldest sister. "Alright, whatever you think is best."

"*Denki*, Nan. And I would appreciate it if you could let Rose know." Aubrey read over Nan's notes, then looked up. "*Denki* for this, too, Nan. You have a gift."

Gift was a generous term for a knack for meddling, Nan thought, as she set off to find her other sister.

The growing cloud cover lent an eerie color to the dusk sky, reminding her again of Reuben's concerns. But she didn't want to dwell on that. Not on her sister's wedding day.

What she really wanted was to set things right with Reuben. She'd like to see that smile of his return. And maybe even hear a real laugh from him. With the right incentive, he might just stay for the singing. What's more, he might even enjoy it. Wishful thinking on her part perhaps, but she was learning that Reuben was full of surprises.

Her new goal was to see Reuben enjoy life a little more. Surely, he wasn't born so sour. Whatever happened to break his spirit, he deserved another chance at happiness. Didn't everyone?

Reuben's fingers curled around his fork as he pushed around the contents of the salad bowl in front of him. The noise level in the room had risen to a pitch that made his shoulders tense. Why there had to be two such elaborate meals in one day, he'd never understand.

Weddings were sacred—a once-in-a-lifetime event for the newlyweds. *Ya*, he knew the reasons, sure enough. Even so, it seemed redundant to him, unlike Nan, who practically bubbled with enthusiasm beside him. She'd probably go for a third round, if she was in charge of tradition.

He stifled a grunt.

"I realize this wedding business isn't exactly in your comfort zone," Jake said from beside him on the left, while Nan was seated to his right. "*Denki* for being here."

Reuben managed a nod, guilt pricking at him. Being asked

to serve his cousin as a side-sitter should be an honor, and he was making it seem like a miserable duty.

"You're the closest family I have now. I couldn't be happier that you've found a perfect home and *frau* for yourself in Promise." And that was the truth, in spite of his mood.

Jake gave him a look and opened his mouth to say something, but Reuben knew that look.

"Don't even." Reuben shook his head at his cousin. "I'm happy for you. Truly. But I know how you besotted folk are always so sure the rest of us are about to find our one and only, as well. Let's not go there. Just enjoy your moment."

Jake grinned back and raised an eyebrow in Nan's direction but kept silent.

Reuben sighed. Even his own cousin was getting the wrong idea. He was here to help Nan, not weigh her down with ridiculous rumors. "No one could be worse for a woman than me, Jake. You wouldn't wish that on your new sister-in-law. Let it go."

"Suit yourself." Jake shrugged, but his smile never dimmed, and Reuben decided to give him a pass. This one time, since it was the man's wedding day. But after this, he'd be sure to squash any such notions.

"Now may not be the time or place for this discussion." Jake leaned closer to be heard. "But Vernon Mast caught wind of some of your concerns, and he believes your fears about catastrophic flooding are well-founded. Might be a good idea to talk to him, if you get the chance."

"Ya," Reuben agreed. As the director of the Mennonite Aid Society, the bishop from Harrisonburg would have insight. "I was hoping to get the chance to speak with him."

Worry lines creased Jake's brow. "This sure is poor timing for a wedding trip. I ought to be here, if bad weather is coming." His cousin worked for the same relief organization. Reuben regretted the cloud hanging over the day for Jake.

"There's no emergency yet, cousin. You only get married once, after all. Storms come and go all the time." Reuben pushed down the intensity of his own worry in an effort to ease Jake's predicament.

A young server—Bethany Weaver, whose father owned the local Amish grocery—interrupted them. "May I take your salad bowl?"

"Ya, denki." He'd barely touched it and was glad the main course would be coming soon.

The girl moved on, and Reuben found his gaze drawn to the windows. The sky had taken on the peculiar greenish cast that often preceded a storm. He wondered if anyone else noticed, or if they were all too caught up in the celebration.

"Pass the potatoes?" Nan's voice startled him from his weather watching.

The sleeve of her blue dress brushed his arm as Nan leaned forward to pass a bowl of steaming whipped potatoes down the table. Her movements and interactions both with him and those around them were so natural—she belonged here among these people in a way he never would. The thought should have reinforced his decision to leave after the meal, but instead it left an unexpected ache in his chest.

He reached for the serving bowl, careful not to let their fingers brush as he took it from her. But she didn't immediately release it, and he was forced to meet her eyes.

"I'm sorry about earlier," she said quietly. "I didn't mean—"

"*Ya*, me, too." This wasn't a conversation he wished to have with every eye on them. But he'd been rash and abrasive with her and already regretted it, so he nodded and attempted a smile to communicate—something of an apology. It was a pitiful attempt, he knew. Likely more frightening than apologetic.

But her eyes softened with relief, anyway, doing strange things to his heart.

"Nan!" John Beachy's voice carried across the room. "How about passing some of that bread near you down this way?"

Reuben's jaw clenched. He could feel the eyes of several guests on them, waiting to see how Nan would respond. Without thinking, he let Nan continue holding the potatoes and picked up the breadbasket himself and passed it in the opposite direction from John.

A soft laugh escaped Nan. "Guess it's going the long way around," she murmured, as he finally took the potatoes from her.

The corner of his mouth twitched despite himself. She had a way of catching him off guard, of making him forget—just for a moment—all the reasons he needed to keep his distance.

A loud clap of thunder rattled the windows, making several guests jump. Conversations paused briefly before resuming with nervous laughter. But Reuben noticed how Nan's eyes met his with understanding. She'd been listening earlier when he'd voiced his concerns, really listening.

"Should we be worried?" she asked softly as a bowl of homemade applesauce and a heaping platter of meat loaf made its way down the table.

He shook his head slightly. "Not yet. But if the time comes…" He hesitated, not wanting to frighten her but needing her to understand. "Promise me you'll take heed if things worsen and your *datt* asks you to wait out the storm at your grandmother's farm. Don't get caught in town or at home." Reuben kept his voice low, though the general din of conversation would have covered it, anyway. "You'll be safer with your family here. This farm is well situated and less likely to flood."

Their eyes met, and something in her expression made his chest tighten. She didn't dismiss his concern or laugh it off as others might have. Instead, she gave a slight nod, her blue eyes serious.

"I promise." She spooned applesauce onto her plate, then added, "If you promise to actually stay for the singing."

He opened his mouth to refuse, but she continued serving and passing the food as if she hadn't just challenged him, as if she hadn't noticed the way his breath caught at her request. The delicious aroma of fried chicken filled his nose as the platter reached him, and he focused on serving himself rather than responding.

But when he glanced at Nan again, he caught the hint of a smile playing at her lips. She knew exactly how she affected him, and worse yet, he wasn't entirely sure he minded.

The meal continued, dishes passing between them in a choreographed dance of tradition. More than once, Reuben caught himself watching Nan's hands—graceful and sure as she spoke between bites and paid attention to others' needs. She had a way of making everyone around her feel at ease, even him. Especially him, if he was honest.

And that had always been the heart of his trouble with the bishop's youngest daughter. He knew she believed he avoided her because he didn't like her much. How wrong she was. He avoided her for her own sake.

When the dessert plates arrived, Nan turned to him with a brightness in her eyes that made him momentarily forget his worries. "I hear Cassie made your favorite—peanut butter pie."

"How did you know that was my favorite?"

"I notice things." She smiled, and for a moment the noise of the crowd faded away. "Like how you always order a slice when you stop at the bakery, even though you pretend you're just there for coffee."

Of course he didn't dare admit that he only stopped at the bakery when he knew she was working there. Still, he found himself returning her smile, marveling at how she'd managed to see past his carefully constructed walls without him realizing it.

But the moment shattered as voices from behind him caught his attention.

"—from Lancaster, *ya*? The Bender boy who thought he knew better than tradition—"

"Heard there was quite the scandal when—"

Reuben's spine stiffened. He didn't need to turn to know Dan Beachy was among those speaking. John's father had connections in Lancaster, and Reuben had noticed him cornering various bishops throughout the afternoon.

Nan must have sensed the change in him. "Reuben?"

He pushed back from the table, the legs of his chair scraping against the floor. The younger folks were already filtering out toward the barn for the evening's events, while older guests said their goodbyes. The perfect time to make an exit.

"I should go." The words felt like gravel in his throat.

"But you promised—"

"*Nay*, Nan. I promised to see you through this supper and see you home. But you're not going home, as you already said." He stood, unable to meet the hurt in her eyes. "It's better for you this way. You shouldn't be associated with someone like me."

"Someone like you?" Her voice held a challenge. "And what sort of person would that be?"

He finally looked at her then, wishing he could explain everything—about Lancaster, about his failures, about why he kept himself apart. But he could already see whispers spreading through the room like ripples in a pond. He wouldn't drag her into the undertow of his past.

"I'm sorry, Nan." He turned away before he could change his mind.

The evening air hit his face like a slap as he stepped outside. The wind had picked up, carrying the scent of rain. He told himself the heaviness in his chest was just concern about the weather, but he knew better.

He should've known he couldn't participate in normal life,

even for one evening. Some mistakes left marks that couldn't be erased, no matter how far you ran or how hard you tried to start over.

Regret stabbed him as he walked his horse to the spot where he'd parked his buggy—a two-seater he had no business keeping. But he'd cleaned it up especially for escorting Nan home tonight. He was a fool.

"Reuben, may I have a quick word?" A deep, authoritative, yet unalarming, voice called to him.

Reuben turned to face Bishop Vernon Mast, his cousin's boss at the Mennonite Aid Society. "Of course," he replied, holding his horse steady. "What can I do for you?"

"Answer a few questions, is all. I'd like to hear your thoughts about this weather we've been having. Naaman tells me you have some legitimate concerns."

"*Ya*, I believe so." Reuben found it easy to speak with Vernon. As Jake had said, the bishop's experience with natural disasters made him a keen listener.

Vernon appeared thoughtful, rubbing his chin for a few moments after Reuben answered his questions. "I wonder if you'd be willing to step in if needed. Jake will be gone, and I may need a man to fill his shoes."

Reuben stifled a mocking laugh. "Jake's shoes are more than I could fill. I'm not able to work with people like he does." In fact, Reuben was growing more uncomfortable with the notion by the second and wishing he'd made it to his buggy a little faster.

"I understand." Vernon's hand cupped around Reuben's shoulder. And to his surprise, the touch was calming rather than off-putting. "I wouldn't expect you to do the same as Jake. Just consider being available to do what you can in his absence. And of course, pray such is not needed after all."

Vernon paused, then added with a chuckle. "No doubt that last part suits you fine."

"It does. I'd rather not be needed for everyone's sake. But I will certainly do all within my ability if the need arises."

Vernon gave his shoulder a firm pat, then dropped his hand. "*Denki*, Reuben, for sharing your wisdom and your willingness to do your part."

As Vernon headed back toward the crowd, the tension that had plagued Reuben for weeks eased. Somewhat, at least. Two bishops had taken his concerns seriously. He'd done what he could to warn people about the threat ahead, and truly there was little else he could do.

Still, he longed for the peace and comfort of his library. To be alone after such a long day was reward enough for stepping so far out of his comfort zone. At least it always had been before.

But then behind him, singing began to drift from the barn, and he had to quicken his pace to outrun the temptation to go back. To be with Nan just a little longer.

Echoes of song mixed with the growing wind, and he hoped the sound wouldn't follow him all the way home.

It did.

Thunder growled in the distance as Reuben approached his empty house, but it wasn't the storm that worried him most. It was how much he'd enjoyed Nan's company all day and knowing that the longer he remained by her side, the more his past would cast shadows on her future.

And now, for the first time in years, solitude brought him no peace. The strum of rainfall against the metal roof above him only served to emphasize the loneliness crowding his soul.

Chapter Five

Three days after the wedding, Nan arrived to work at Cassie's bakery the same as she always did on Saturday mornings. But this morning, she found Cassie frantically readying a large bread order for Weaver's Amish Grocer.

"Another delivery already?" Nan jumped in to help and pulled the last batch of golden brown loaves from the oven. The scent of fresh bread filled the bakery's kitchen, but something felt off about needing a second order so early. Even at the peak of the fall foliage tourist season, Nick Weaver didn't run out of bread this quickly. And peak season wasn't for weeks yet.

"Uncle Nick sent word with Bethany to make more before I finished the first batch early this morning." Cassie wiped the flour from her hands. "He's never seen anything like it."

"But it's only nine o'clock." Nan began arranging the warm loaves in delivery baskets. Usually the Amish grocer's Saturday bread order lasted at least through lunch on a busy day.

"*Ya*, I know. If I'd gotten a chance, I'd have sent you word to come sooner. *Onkel* Nick said there was a line waiting for him as soon as he opened the doors this morning. That wiped him out of yesterday's leftover stock. And there were more customers lined up to buy the morning supply as soon as I could get them ready."

The bell above the shop door chimed, and Bethany Weaver hurried in from the retail area. Nick's teenage daughter was flushed, her *kapp* slightly askew. "The wind is whipping up something fierce out there." She tidied her *kapp* hurriedly. "*Mamm* sent me to help with deliveries. The store is packed."

"Packed?" Cassie's eyebrows rose. "With who? Promise isn't that big."

"Everyone." Bethany grabbed an empty basket. "All the *Englisch* from town are buying up bread, canned goods, matches—anything they can get their hands on. *Datt* had to limit how many loaves each family could take."

A niggle of unease worked its way up Nan's spine. "Did anyone say why?"

"Something about a hurricane coming up from Florida." Bethany shrugged. "I heard Mr. Nicely from the gas station telling *Datt* it could be bad. But we don't get hurricanes in the mountains." She glanced at Nan. "Do we?"

Nan's hands stilled on the bread she was wrapping. She'd said those exact words to Reuben at the wedding. He had known something she didn't, for sure.

The bell chimed again. Through the kitchen doorway, Nan could see several customers enter, speaking in hushed, urgent tones.

"We should stock up," one woman said. "The forecast changed. They're saying it made a turn straight for the mountains. We're in for more rain and high winds, too. Doesn't sound good to me."

"My grandma still talks about when the remnants of Hurricane Agnes dumped over ten inches of rain here." Her companion was shaking her head. "She lost everything in that flood."

What had Reuben said about wind and water being even worse? To pray we don't get a hurricane. She swallowed against the growing lump of anxiety in her throat and turned to face Bethany, now wide-eyed after overhearing the same comments.

This wasn't the time to fret. They had work to do.

Nan gently placed a hand on Bethany's arm to show her support. "We will get prepared, too. I'll come with you to deliver this bread, and then I need to update my father."

Bethany nodded, though her eyes still darted with uncertainty toward the customers.

"*Gott* will help us, Bethany." Nan spoke the words as much to reassure herself as the frightened *youngie*.

"Nan is right. You should both go quickly," Cassie chimed in. "There's only so much *goot* we can do here, but the bishop needs to know right away."

"I'll be back," Nan assured Cassie, glancing at all that was left to be done. Her friend had been so busy with the bread, she hadn't begun to restock her own supplies.

"*Nay*, at this rate, we'll all be sold out soon, no matter how much we produce." Cassie's calm, common sense took over. "Your *datt* will need your help more than I do. And Bethany, you can send someone to fetch Martin. He'll take care of me."

Nan gathered her shawl, her mind already racing ahead. Reuben had known—had tried to warn them all. He'd seen this coming, and now he was probably holed up in that library of his, blissfully unaware his predictions were unfolding before their eyes.

The thought riled her into action. She and Bethany worked in tandem, loading the racks of bread into bins on the back of Nick Weaver's wagon. The ride from the bakery to the grocery was less than a half mile, but long enough for Nan to calculate a plan.

"Was *Datt* at the store when you left?" she asked Bethany, knowing he often made his way there in the mornings to play checkers on the front porch with customers.

"*Ya*, the bishop and a growing crowd of farmers. More than usual, but that seems to be the trend today." Bethany hurried the horse down the lane. She was a capable driver, hardly a little girl anymore, as Nan sometimes still thought of her.

Nan's *datt* would already be aware of the weather forecast if he was at the store interacting with the others growing concerned. He didn't need her warning, not since Reuben had already informed him of what could happen. And for sure, he'd send her straight to her *grossmammi*'s farm. She'd hurry there soon to make sure *Grossmammi* and the rest of the family at the farmhouse were prepared, especially with the children there while Aubrey and Jake were away. She had promised Reuben she would go when asked, but she couldn't. Not yet. She had something more important to do.

"Might you consider doing me a favor, then?" She spoke above the increasing wind to Bethany, who nodded back in agreement.

"After we get the bread unloaded, I must hurry. Can you let my father know that I've gone to recruit Reuben's help? Tell him that I will go straight to the sunflower farm afterward and wait for him, as I know he will want me to do. But Reuben's farm is not so far out of the way." Conveniently. If it was, she'd have traveled in the opposite direction, anyway.

"Reuben?" Bethany's eyes widened. "But he never—"

"That's exactly the problem." Nan straightened her shoulders. "He's capable of helping us all right now. And this time, he's not going to hide away..." She caught herself before revealing his library. "Not if I have anything to say about it."

As soon as she helped Bethany unload the bread order, she'd be on her way to rouse Reuben from his hideaway. Whatever happened before he'd come to Promise—things she'd only heard through unreliable gossip and always vague—he'd hidden long enough.

Promise needed him. Surely, he'd understand that, now.

Bethany pulled the horse to a stop by the back door of the store out of sight of customers. But not unseen, apparently.

"Nan," the unmistakable voice of her father called from behind. And Nan felt her carefully laid plans to get to Reuben dissolve. "I was on my way to the bakery to find you."

Her *datt* held the lead reins of her favorite horse, a rescue animal who never pulled a buggy but was her faithful trail companion on horseback through the hills. "I brought Buttercup with me. She'll serve you better in this weather than your bicycle, and you can ride over to your *grossmammi*'s farm without me. You'll all be safe there, but I must warn our farmers who haven't heard."

"Ach, Datt—"

"*Nay*, *dochter*, no arguments this time. Be kind to your old *datt* and free my mind from this one worry. I must know you are safe."

Tears stung at the back of her eyes. She'd never doubted her *datt*'s love, but the intensity in his gaze and the tremble of his voice was almost more than she could bear. "So it is truly as bad as they're saying?"

"Worse, I fear. The creek's already rising from rains upstream, and this is only the beginning." He nodded gravely. "I've sent word to *Grossmammi* to prepare the farmhouse. You should head there directly—they'll need your help."

"But what about you?" Nan felt a familiar twist of worry. "You won't try to check on the outlying farms alone, will you?"

Her *datt* sighed. "Someone must warn those who haven't heard. The Millers, the Schrocks—they're all too far from town to know what's coming."

"Then I should come with you—"

"Nay, dochter." His voice was firm. "I need to know you're safe at the farmhouse with our family. Promise me you'll go straight there."

She'd made the same promise once before to Reuben. But how could she have known how she'd really feel in such a situation? "I just want to do the right thing, *Datt*."

"Helping your family at the farm and staying safe is the right thing, Nan." He squeezed her hand. "I'll join you at the farmhouse before dark. Now go, before the roads become worse."

Nan hesitated, glancing around at the crowded store. "*Datt*, what about Reuben? Has anyone warned him? He could… He'd help you. I know he would, and you wouldn't be alone."

A strange look crossed her father's face. "Reuben knows. In fact, he was the one to warn me. He came to the house just minutes after you left earlier. But he's already gone…" Her father paused. "He's gone to warn some of the families to the north."

Something in her *datt*'s manner made Nan uneasy. He didn't deny the danger—to himself or to Reuben. The resulting worry for her father wasn't surprising, of course. But why did the thought of Reuben out alone in the storm make her heart clench so painfully?

"I should go," she said abruptly, suddenly eager to get to the farmhouse. Keeping her promise was about all she knew to do, now, while her heart was being torn in so many directions.

As Nan rode away, the sky darkened overhead. The wind picked up, sending leaves skittering across her path and tugging at her *kapp*. She urged her horse faster, trying to outrun the sense of foreboding that grew with each passing minute.

Reuben had been right all along. And somehow, she knew this storm would change everything.

Reuben leaned forward in his saddle, urging Solomon, his reliable and sturdy mule, through the thickening storm. The wind tore at his hat, and fat raindrops splattered against his oilskin coat. His thoughts kept turning to the bishop—and to Nan.

He'd helped warn the Millers in their northwestern hollow, but by the time he'd reached them, the creek was already spilling its banks. They'd gathered what they could and headed for higher ground at their cousin's place on the ridge.

Now, as Reuben made his way back toward town, he wondered if he should have gone straight to the Burkholders' sunflower farm instead. Bishop Naaman was out checking on the southeastern farms—they'd divided the territory between them earlier that morning, when the forecast had gone from concerning to dire.

"*Ach*, she's safe by now," he muttered to his horse, trying to convince himself more than the animal. Her *datt* had gone to find her first and was confident she'd go straight to the farmhouse.

But the nagging worry persisted. He knew Nan too well. Her promise to him might have been sincere in the moment, but if she thought someone needed help…

The rain intensified, pounding against his shoulders. Visibility dropped to mere yards ahead. Solomon balked at a fallen branch, nearly unseating him. Lightning cracked overhead, followed immediately by a thunder boom that shook the very ground.

"Easy," he soothed the frightened animal. "*Gott* is with us."

The words felt hollow in his mouth. Hadn't he said similar words to his family in Lancaster, before disaster struck? The memories surged back. Reuben shook his head, trying to clear the visions.

This was different. A natural disaster. Not a man-made catastrophe resulting from his pride and push for modern equipment. And he'd warned people in time. He'd done what he could.

Still, as he approached the fork in the road—one path leading toward town, the other toward his farm and library—he hesitated. Logic said to head for his farm. The buildings were on high ground, and he'd prepared supplies. He'd be safe there until the worst passed.

But something pulled him toward the Burkholders' farm on the opposite hill. Just to be certain Nan had made it safely. Just to ease his mind.

"Foolishness," he growled, even as he guided his mule toward the Burkholders' place. The animal struggled against the wind, head lowered in determination that matched his own.

A flash of movement caught his eye—a horse and rider cutting across the lower meadow. His heart stopped. Even through the driving rain, he'd recognize that silhouette anywhere.

Nan.

But she wasn't tucked away at the farmhouse on the hill. She was riding away from the farm.

Panic surged through him. The meadow she was crossing would be underwater within the hour if the rain continued at this pace. Without a thought, Reuben changed course, urging his reluctant mule off the relative safety of the road and into the open field.

"Nan!" he shouted, but the wind stole his voice. He pressed forward, fighting the elements.

Part of him—the rational, self-preserving part—argued that this was exactly why he'd chosen solitude. Caring for others meant risking everything, meant facing the possibility of failing them. Just as he'd failed before.

But a stronger voice inside him, one that had been silenced for too long, refused to let him turn away. Not this time.

Rain-soaked and breathless, he finally caught up to her.

"Nan!" This time, the wind carried his voice to her. She turned, her face a mixture of surprise and relief.

"Reuben! What are you doing here?" Her surprise was evident as he hurried his mule closer to her.

"I could ask you the same!" He maneuvered his animal alongside hers. "You promised you'd go to the farmhouse!"

Lightning illuminated her determined expression. "I did! But *Datt* hasn't returned. The bridge at Stoney Creek might be washed out already. I have to find him!"

Reuben felt a chill that had nothing to do with the rain. "Nan, we need to get to higher ground. Now. This meadow isn't safe."

As if to punctuate his words, thunder cracked overhead, causing both animals to snort in fear. Nan's mount reared slightly, and she clutched at the saddle horn to keep her seat.

"I'm not turning back until I find my *datt*!" Her blue eyes flashed with a stubbornness he recognized all too well.

Reuben took a deep breath. "Then I'm coming with you." The decision settled in his chest with surprising rightness. "But we need to be smart about this."

Relief softened her features. "You'll help me find him?"

"Ya." Reuben nodded, already calculating their best route. "But you follow my lead. No arguments."

For once, Nan simply nodded, the gravity of the situation apparent even to her headstrong nature.

"We'll try the old logging road," he said, pointing east. "It runs higher than the main path. If the bridge is out, your *datt* might have taken shelter at the Yoder sawmill."

As they turned their horses, Reuben felt the familiar weight of responsibility settle on his shoulders. But this time, it didn't come with the usual dread. Instead, he felt…purposeful.

They rode side by side into the worsening storm, neither speaking what both were thinking: they might already be too late.

Chapter Six

The logging road narrowed before them, dirt giving way to mud that sucked at their animals' hooves. Reuben's mule, accustomed to his weight, trudged forward with determination. Behind him, Nan's horse struggled more, its steps hesitant on the increasingly treacherous path.

Rain that had been falling steadily now drove sideways, stinging Reuben's face and hands. He pulled his hat lower, though it provided little protection against the onslaught. The wind had picked up dramatically in the last fifteen minutes, bending the tops of the tall pines until they swayed like wheat in a summer breeze—only there was nothing gentle about this movement.

"We should find shelter soon," he called back to Nan, his voice nearly lost in a growl of thunder.

She urged her horse forward until they rode side by side where the path widened slightly. "Not until we find *Datt*."

The stubbornness in her voice both frustrated and impressed him. He'd never known anyone quite so determined—or so foolhardy. But who was he to judge? Hadn't his own foolishness cost him everything once before?

The memory hit him with the force of the driving rain—the way the water had risen on his family's farm in Lancaster, how he'd insisted they could manage. His modern pumping system would handle it, he'd said. His calculations were sound. And then the power had failed, and the backup generator had stuttered and died, and the rest… The rest was the shame he carried every day.

"Reuben?" Nan's voice cut through his thoughts.

He blinked, realizing his mule had stopped while his mind wandered. "*Ya*, sorry. Just thinking."

"About what?" Her blue eyes studied him with that unsettling perception that always made him feel exposed.

"Nothing that matters now," he muttered, nudging his mule forward.

The scent of saturated earth rose up around them, rich and heavy. Water no longer merely pooled on the ground but ran in small rivulets beneath them, seeking the path of least resistance downhill. Reuben watched a small stream form beside the trail, gathering speed and volume with each passing minute.

Above them, the pines creaked ominously. One particularly old tree bent at an angle that made Reuben's skin crawl with warning.

"Stay to the right," he directed sharply as they approached it.

Nan obeyed without question, moving her horse to the far edge of the path. Not a moment too soon—a sharp crack split the air, and a large branch crashed down where they would have been.

Nan's horse reared, startled by the noise and movement. She clung to its mane, fighting for balance as the animal pranced sideways toward the edge of the path where the ground fell away steeply.

Without thinking, Reuben lunged across the space between them, his hand closing around her arm, steadying her until the horse calmed. Her sleeve was soaked through, and her skin was cold beneath the fabric.

"That was close," she said, her eyes wide but voice steady.

He withdrew his hand quickly, too aware of his powerful

response and uncertain whether she welcomed it or not. "Your horse is spooked. Best to keep moving."

The path climbed steadily for the next quarter mile, leading them to a ridge that offered a view across the valley. Through gaps in the trees and sheets of rain, Reuben could make out the patchwork of fields and farmhouses below.

Something in the air changed. The birds, who had been calling warnings to each other, fell suddenly silent. The pressure dropped, making his ears pop.

"What is it?" Nan asked, noticing his tension.

"I'm not sure. Something's not—"

He stopped mid-sentence. On the opposite ridge, perhaps a half mile away, a patch of earth seemed to ripple, as if the ground itself had become liquid. It started slowly—a small slippage, a few trees tilting—then gathered terrible momentum.

"*Gott im Himmel*, help us!" he murmured a desperate prayer heavenward.

The entire hillside was moving, a river of mud and debris flowing downward toward the farms below. Even from this distance, Reuben could see buildings in its path—barns, outbuildings, perhaps homes.

Beside him, Nan made a small sound—not quite a cry, more like a sharp intake of breath. Her hand moved to her lips in an instinctive gesture. For a moment, she looked as young and vulnerable as the day he'd first seen her, years ago when he'd arrived in Promise.

He wished more than anything he could have protected her from this sight. But even as the thought formed, her expression changed, composure returning to her features though her eyes remained haunted.

"The Yoders' farm is down there," she said, her voice remarkably steady. "And all their kin, too."

Reuben calculated quickly, his mind racing ahead to map

the mudslide's likely path. The destruction would be considerable, but a more urgent thought struck him.

"Which way would your *datt* have gone from here?"

Nan's gaze followed his out over the valley, then to the continuing path ahead. "He may have gone to check on the Hochstetlers. Their place is just beyond that ridge to the north."

Reuben's stomach tightened. If his calculations were correct, the bishop might be dangerously close to the effects of the mudslide.

"We need to hurry." He didn't soften the urgency in his voice.

Nan simply nodded, eyes meeting his with perfect understanding.

Reuben found himself doing something he hadn't done properly in years—praying, not out of obligation or habit, but from the depths of his heart. Bitte, Gott, *let us find him in time. Let us not be too late.*

They pressed on, pushing as fast as was safe on the treacherous ground. Around a bend in the path, Reuben spotted fresh tracks—the unmistakable imprint of buggy wheels and horse hooves, partially filled with water but recent enough to be visible.

"Your *datt* came this way." He pointed to the tracks and prayed they had been left by the bishop. "And not long ago."

Nan's face lit with hope. "Then we keep going."

The rain drove harder against them, but Reuben barely noticed it now. All that mattered was following those tracks before the water washed them away completely. He led the way forward, his senses alert to every sound and movement in the storm-lashed forest around them.

Behind him, he heard Nan murmuring what might have been prayers. And as was becoming more common of late, the sound of her voice brought not irritation but comfort.

Nan's eyes strained through the curtain of rain, desperately scanning the landscape below for any sign of her *datt*. The tracks they followed were becoming fainter with each passing minute as the relentless water washed them away. Her heart hammered against her ribs, matching the thunderclaps that rolled across the sky.

"The storm is worsening. We need to find him soon," Reuben called over his shoulder. "Don't go too far without me. But if I head up this ridge and you go down, we can cover more ground." Fear and regret echoed through his words. Fear for her. Regret at not having found her father yet. "But don't go beyond that giant sycamore without me." He nodded downhill at the landmark.

She continued cautiously and was about to lose hope when something caught her eye—a flash of pale yellow against the brown mud about fifty yards down the slope. Her father's straw hat?

And then beside it, partially obscured by fallen branches and debris, was the unmistakable corner of an overturned buggy.

"Datt!" she screamed, her voice lost in the howling wind.

Without thinking, she dug her heels into her horse's flanks and surged forward, veering off the path toward the wreckage.

"Nan! Stop!" Reuben's voice rang out behind her, but she couldn't wait, couldn't be cautious, not when every second might mean the difference between life and death.

Her horse slipped and slid down the muddy incline, its hooves fighting for purchase on the treacherous ground. Branches whipped at her face and arms as she leaned low over the animal's neck, urging it forward.

If only I'd insisted on going with him this morning. If only I'd been more stubborn. Please, Gott, *please let him be alive.*

She reached the overturned buggy and leaped from her mount, her boots sinking ankle-deep in the mud. The side of the buggy was splintered, one wheel torn completely off.

"Datt?" she called, circling around to where she'd seen the hat.

Her father lay pinned beneath the buggy's frame, mud and water pooling around him. His face was pale, eyes closed, and for one terrible moment, Nan thought she'd arrived too late.

Then his eyelids fluttered open. *"Nan?"* His voice was weak but clear. "*Vas machst du hier?* What are you doing here? You shouldn't have come."

She dropped to her knees beside him, ignoring the cold mud that immediately soaked through her dress. "I'm here now, and we're going to get you out." Her fingers found his hand and clasped it tightly, her own trembling.

"The horse?" he asked.

"I don't see it," she said, glancing around. The buggy horse must have broken free and fled.

Her father grimaced as he tried to shift his position. "My leg is broken, I think. And something…" He winced. "Something inside doesn't feel right."

Nan fought back tears as she assessed the situation. The buggy frame pressed down across her father's lower body, trapping him securely. She braced her shoulder against the wooden frame and pushed with all her might, her boots sliding in the mud, muscles straining. The buggy didn't budge an inch.

"Datt, I can't move it," she admitted, the words catching in her throat.

"You need to go, Nan. Find shelter." His words were punctuated by labored breaths. "The water is rising. This whole area could flood or slide. I've never…never seen the like of it."

"I'm not leaving you." She gripped his hand tighter, as if she could anchor him there by sheer force of will. "Reuben is not far behind me. He'll know what to do."

Even as she spoke, the slosh of mule's hooves in the wet and mud announced Reuben's arrival. He dismounted in one fluid motion and was beside them in seconds, his experienced eyes taking in the scene.

"Bishop Naaman," he acknowledged, his voice instantly

transforming from the hesitant, guarded tone she was accustomed to hearing. This was a different Reuben—focused, authoritative, decisive.

He knelt in the mud beside them, carefully examining where the buggy trapped her father. His hands moved with surprising gentleness as he checked the bishop's pulse and assessed his injuries. Rain streamed down his face, plastering his dark hair to his forehead, but he seemed oblivious to his own discomfort.

"How bad is the pain?" Reuben asked, his fingers probing along her father's side.

"Bearable," her father replied, though the tight lines around his mouth suggested otherwise.

Reuben nodded once, then turned to Nan. "I need you to keep him talking and as still as possible. I'm going to see if I can lever this up enough to pull him free."

He moved with urgent efficiency, searching the surrounding debris until he found a sturdy branch that had broken from one of the trees above. Testing its strength against his knee, he nodded in satisfaction, then positioned it beneath the buggy frame, creating a primitive lever.

"When I lift, you'll need to help pull him clear," Reuben instructed, positioning himself at the branch's end. "Be careful of his leg—try not to twist or bend it."

Nan moved to her father's shoulders, gripping beneath his arms as Reuben had shown her. Her father's eyes met hers, full of pain but also a steadfast trust that gave her strength.

"Ready?" Reuben called.

"Ya," she responded, bracing herself.

Reuben threw his full weight onto the branch. For a heartbeat, nothing happened. Then with a creak of protest, the buggy frame shifted slightly. Reuben's face contorted with effort, muscles straining beneath his soaked shirt as he pushed harder.

The sound of splintering wood cut through the rain as the

buggy's damaged axle finally gave way. The frame lifted just enough.

"Now!" Reuben commanded.

Nan pulled backward, dragging her father from beneath the wreckage. His cry of pain cut through her like a knife, but she didn't stop until he was completely free. The moment they were clear, Reuben released the lever, and the buggy crashed back down, sending up a spray of muddy water.

Reuben was beside them instantly, his hands moving carefully over her father's injured leg. Even to Nan's untrained eye the break was obvious—the unnatural angle, the swelling already visible beneath the torn trouser fabric.

"We need to stabilize this before we move him." Reuben glanced at the sky, then at the rising water around them. "And we need to do it quickly."

Her father reached out and gripped Reuben's arm. "*Denki*, Reuben. *Gott* sent you today."

Something flashed across Reuben's face—surprise, perhaps, or discomfort at the praise. But he nodded before turning back to the buggy wreckage.

Working methodically, he broke off two flat pieces of wood from the buggy's side panel, then tore strips from his own shirt to create bindings. His hands were remarkably deft as he fashioned a splint for her father's leg.

"Where did you learn to do that?" Nan asked, watching in fascination.

"On the farm," he replied without looking up. "Animals get injured. Sometimes there's no time to fetch a vet." He secured the last binding and sat back on his heels. "It's not perfect, but it will keep the bone stable for now."

Her father's face had grown alarmingly pale, and Nan noticed he was shivering despite the relative warmth of the rain.

"He's going into shock," Reuben said, noticing the same signs. "We need to get him somewhere dry and warm."

"*Datt*'s hunting lodge?" Nan suggested, thinking of her father's cabin in the woods where they'd have plenty of food and bunks for sleeping.

Reuben shook his head. "Too far, and we'd have to travel even closer to where the mudslide hit." He looked at the bishop, then back at Nan, indecision briefly crossing his features before resolve settled in. "My library is closest. It's not ideal, but it's our safest and closest option."

"Your library?" her father murmured, his voice weak. "What library?"

"I'll explain later, Bishop," Reuben said. "Right now, we need to focus on getting you there safely."

He turned to the buggy again, this time breaking apart the front seat and frame. Working quickly, he constructed a makeshift stretcher. *Nay*, it was a sled appearing before her eyes as he lashed the pieces together with leather reins from the bishop's harness. Nan watched him work, amazed at his ingenuity.

"Will it hold him?" she asked when he'd finished.

"It has to." Reuben tested the joins one last time. "My mule is stronger—he'll pull the sled. You can lead yours and carry what supplies we can salvage."

Together they transferred her father onto the sled-like gurney, covering him with Reuben's coat. Though he tried to hide it, the movement clearly caused her father intense pain. By the time they finished, his eyes were closed again, his breathing shallow.

"*Datt?* Stay with us," Nan urged, squeezing his hand.

His eyes fluttered open. "I'm here, *liebling*. Just need to rest a moment."

Reuben attached the sled to his mule's harness, speaking soothingly to the animal. "The rain's getting harder," he observed, looking up at the darkening sky. "We need to move now."

"Wait," her father called weakly. "My Bible. In the buggy box."

Nan looked to Reuben, who nodded. With no explanation needed, he waded through the deepening water to the overturned buggy. He retrieved the small, worn Bible from the waterproof box that had remarkably stayed intact.

"Anything else?" he asked, scanning the wreckage.

Her father shook his head slightly. "That's all that matters."

Reuben handed the Bible to Nan, who tucked it securely inside her dress. She gathered the reins of her horse while Reuben carefully checked the sled one last time.

"It's about a mile to my place," he told her. "The terrain is rough, and the rain isn't helping. We'll need to go slowly for his sake, but as quickly as we can before the water rises further."

As if for emphasis, a new stream suddenly appeared from higher on the hill, cutting across their path with surprising force.

"Let's go," Nan said, her resolve hardening. She looked down at her father's pale face. "We're going to get you somewhere safe, *Datt*. Just hold on."

They set off through the rain, Reuben leading his mule with the makeshift sled while Nan followed, one hand on her own horse's reins, the other alternating between steadying the sled and reaching down to touch her father's shoulder. Behind them, water continued to pool and flow down the hill, erasing their tracks and the evidence of the accident as if it had never happened.

Her father's eyes opened and closed, consciousness coming and going. During one lucid moment, he looked up at the sky, rain falling on his face, and whispered words Nan barely caught: "*Der Herr ist mein Hirte*... The Lord is my shepherd."

"Mir mangelt nichts," Nan continued automatically. "I shall not want."

"He maketh me to lie down in green pastures," her father murmured. "He leadeth me beside the still waters."

The familiar psalm, recited in such dire circumstances, brought tears to Nan's eyes. But it also brought strength. Her father had always been her rock. Now it was her turn to be strong for him.

Ahead, Reuben paused as they reached a small gully that had transformed into a rushing stream. "We'll need to cross quickly," he called back to her. "The water's rising fast."

He surveyed the area, then pointed to a spot where a narrow strip of uncovered land spanned the gap. "We can cross there, but I'll have to carry the bishop. Do you think you can guide the animals through the water?"

Nan nodded, moving forward to help. As she reached Reuben's side, their hands brushed briefly. Despite the cold and wet, she felt a warmth in that momentary contact—a reminder that she wasn't facing this alone.

"We'll get him to safety," Reuben said quietly, his amber eyes meeting hers with surprising gentleness. "I promise, Nan."

In that moment, she believed him completely.

Reuben's arms ached with the effort of carrying the bishop across the rushing water. They'd feared the crossing on the sled was too risky, so Reuben had lifted the bishop himself. He cradled the older man against his chest, each step careful and measured as he found footholds on the rocky patches beneath the surging water.

Behind him, Nan rode her horse while guiding Solomon along with a lead rope. Her blond hair was plastered to her face, blue eyes wide with determination as she navigated the watery crossing. The horse moved carefully, sensing the danger, while the mule followed with characteristic stubbornness. Despite everything—the danger, the rain, her father's condition—Nan hadn't faltered once. Not since that first moment of finding her father trapped.

Once across the stream, they carefully repositioned the bishop onto the sled behind Reuben's mule. They continued toward Reuben's property on higher ground, the trees growing denser, offering some meager shelter from the relentless downpour. The familiar path to his library appeared ahead, though the storm had transformed it into something barely recognizable. Reuben knew they couldn't risk traveling the rest of the way to his cabin. At this point, the library truly was their only option.

"Almost there," he called back to Nan.

Even as he spoke, the bishop's breathing changed—becoming more labored, the gaps between breaths stretching worryingly long. Reuben halted, kneeling swiftly beside the sled.

"What's wrong?" Nan was at his side instantly, her hand finding her father's.

"His breathing's changed." Reuben placed his palm lightly on the bishop's chest, feeling the irregular rise and fall. "Could be pain from a broken rib. Let's pray his lungs have not been injured. I can bind him better when we get to the library."

The shadow that crossed Nan's face told him she understood the gravity of what he wasn't saying—that their careful transport might not be enough, that despite everything they'd done, his injuries may have worsened.

For a heartbeat, he saw her faith waver—saw the flicker of hopelessness threaten to take hold.

"Nan." He took her hand without thinking, his larger one engulfing her cold fingers. "We can still help him. But we need to hurry."

She nodded, squeezing his hand once before letting go. The momentary connection left him unbalanced—as if he'd offered her strength only to find she'd given him some of her own in return.

They reached his library just as the light began to fade from the sky. The stone and timber sanctuary looked unchanged amid the chaos of the storm, a testament to its builders' skill centuries ago and Reuben's careful restoration. Never had he been so grateful for its solid walls.

Getting the bishop inside proved another challenge. Rather than jostle the bishop from his makeshift bed once more, Reuben and Nan carefully lifted the sled and carried him up the steps. The bishop's weight was substantial, but Nan bore her portion without complaint, though her arms trembled with the strain.

Inside, the air was still and dry, the remnants of that morning's fire for his coffee providing a hint of warmth. Reuben had not intended to return until the storm passed, had not anticipated bringing anyone—especially not Nan—back to his private sanctuary. Yet here they were.

He cleared space near the fire, pushing aside books and papers. Together, they lowered the bishop onto the thick rug that covered the stone floor.

"Get the fire going," he instructed Nan. "There's wood stacked beneath the overhang on the back porch. Hopefully some is still dry. He needs warmth."

While Nan tended to the fire, Reuben checked the bishop's vital signs again. The pulse beneath his fingertips was thready and weak, the skin clammy despite the sweat beading on the older man's brow. The possibility of internal bleeding worried him most—a problem far beyond his limited medical knowledge.

"Reuben," the bishop murmured, his eyes opening to focus on him with surprising clarity.

"Save your strength," Reuben replied, uncomfortable with the intensity of the man's gaze.

"Nay." The bishop's hand found his wrist, the grip surprisingly strong. "Listen to me. If I don't make it—"

"You will." Reuben cut him off, unwilling to hear what might follow.

"If I don't," the bishop insisted, "you must take care of her."

Reuben froze, the words striking him like a physical blow. "Bishop, I—"

"Promise me." The grip on his wrist tightened. "Promise me you'll see her safely home when this passes. That you won't leave her alone."

Before Reuben could respond, Nan returned with an armful of firewood. "The wood's a bit damp," she reported, "but I found some dry pieces underneath." She knelt beside her father, her forehead creasing with concern as she noted his pallor. "How is he?"

Reuben met the bishop's eyes once more, seeing the question there—the demand for his word. He gave a short nod, a promise made without Nan's knowledge.

"He needs dry clothes and medicine for the pain," Reuben said, standing abruptly. "I don't have much here, but there's a chest in the back with some supplies."

He moved away, grateful for the excuse to put distance between himself and the intensity of emotions that threatened to overwhelm him. The bishop's request echoed in his mind. *Take care of her. Don't leave her alone.*

How could he make such a promise? He, who had failed everyone who ever depended on him.

At the back of the library, he paused before an old trunk, his hands resting on its worn leather surface. Inside were the remnants of his former life—clothes, a few personal items, medicines he'd brought from Lancaster. Things he kept but rarely used, reminders of what he'd lost. Of the day of the Lancaster flood that had destroyed everything—his farm, his reputation, his confidence. And the day he'd learned that all his knowledge wasn't enough when it really mattered.

A soft sound made him turn. Nan stood a few feet away, her eyes wide and questioning. He hadn't heard her approach.

"He's asking for you," she said simply.

Reuben nodded, unable to find words. He opened the trunk, pulling out dry clothing and a small medical kit.

"We'll do what we can," he said, his voice rough. "But Nan,

you should know… I've been in a situation like this before. And I—" He swallowed hard. "I failed everyone."

The confession hung between them in the quiet library, punctuated only by the crackling fire and the steady drum of rain on the roof.

Nan took a step closer, close enough that he could see the flecks of darker blue in her eyes, the faint freckles across her nose usually unnoticeable.

"Then, this time we put our confidence in *Gott*, *ya*?" How could she understand so easily his precise failing point? That he'd done things his way, instead of relying on *Gott*. Humbled, he could only nod in agreement as she continued. "We have no choice but to pray that *Gott* guides you this time," she said softly. "Because my *datt* needs you. And I…" Her voice faltered. "I need you, too."

Something shifted in Reuben's chest—something long frozen beginning to crack and thaw. He gathered the supplies and followed her back to where her father lay waiting.

Outside the library walls, the storm intensified, the wind howling with renewed fury. The sound of a massive crack followed by a thunderous crash told him another tree had fallen nearby. They were trapped here, for better or worse.

As Reuben knelt beside the bishop once more, he made another silent promise—not just to the injured man before him, but to himself and to *Gott*.

Both a promise and a prayer—that this time would be different.

Chapter Seven

The fire crackled and popped as it consumed the dry wood Nan had found stacked neatly beside Reuben's stone fireplace. The flames cast dancing shadows across the walls of books surrounding them, their spines standing like silent sentinels in the warm glow.

Her father lay on a thick rug near the fire, his breathing labored but steadier than it had been during their harrowing journey. Nan wrung out a cloth in a basin of water and gently wiped his brow. His eyes fluttered open briefly at her touch, then closed again.

"Does that feel better, *Datt*?" she asked softly.

He managed a slight nod, the movement barely perceptible.

Behind her, Reuben moved about the library with quiet efficiency, gathering supplies and arranging them on a small table he'd pulled close to where her father rested. Watching him from the corner of her eye, Nan marveled at how different he seemed here, in his private sanctuary. The perpetual tension that usually marked his posture had eased somewhat, replaced by a focused determination.

"The tea water should be hot soon," Reuben said, checking the kettle he'd hung over the fire. "I have some herbs that might help with the pain."

"Denki, Reuben." Nan turned her attention back to her father, trying to mask her surprise.

For sure, she never would have guessed that Reuben knew or cared about the medicinal properties of herbs. But Reuben was proving more than capable of helping with her father, far beyond the heavy lifting required to get him to safety.

The binding they'd wrapped around his chest seemed to have helped a little. Reuben had suggested it might stabilize any broken ribs and ease his breathing. The process of binding had been difficult—her father barely conscious, his face contorting with pain at each slight movement—but worth it for the small improvement it brought.

She still felt a flutter of surprise when she recalled how Reuben had hesitated before tearing the crisp white shirt he'd pulled from an old wooden chest. His large hands had paused, fingering the fine fabric for a heartbeat before he'd ripped it decisively into strips.

"Are you sure?" she'd asked. "That looks like good material."

His amber eyes had met hers, something unfathomable in their depths. "No material is more important than the worth of a real, living person."

The emphasis he'd placed on the word *living* caught her attention, as did the shadow that crossed his features. But his expression had shuttered immediately, closing off whatever emotion had briefly surfaced.

Now, as she adjusted the binding around her father's chest, she wondered again about what lay behind those words. So much about Reuben remained a mystery.

The kettle began to whistle, and Reuben moved it from the fire. He mixed dried herbs into a mug, then poured the steaming water over them. The fragrant aroma of chamomile and something else—turmeric, perhaps—filled the air. Reuben truly understood the use of herbal mixes for medicinal teas. How had she missed that bit of knowledge about him, when teas were her specialty?

"This will help with the pain and might induce sleep," Reuben explained as he handed the mug to Nan. "He needs rest to heal."

"*Ya*, it will, for sure." Nan nodded gratefully, then turned back to her father. "Can you drink a little, *Datt*?"

She supported his head with one hand while bringing the mug to his lips with the other. He managed a few small sips, exhaustion evident in every line of his face.

"You're safe now," she assured him, gently lowering his head back to the folded blanket that served as a pillow. "We're going to take good care of you."

Her father's eyes opened slightly. *"Nan,"* he whispered. His hand reached for hers, his grip surprisingly strong despite his condition. "Promise me...you'll listen to Reuben. Trust him."

Nan glanced up at Reuben, who stood a few paces away, his expression unreadable. Their eyes met briefly before he looked away, busying himself with organizing supplies.

"I will, *Datt*," she answered, though uncertainty stirred within her. Trust Reuben? The man who had kept himself apart from their community, who guarded his privacy like a miser hoarded gold? And yet, hadn't he already proven himself today?

She watched as Reuben moved to the window, peering out into the darkness. The rain still beat against the glass, though it seemed to have lessened somewhat from the earlier downpour.

"I need to try to reach my cabin," he said without turning around. "There are supplies there—more bandages, medicine, food. Things we'll need if we're trapped here for more than a day."

"In this weather?" Nan protested. "It's not safe."

"It's not far." He finally turned to face her. "And the rain is letting up. If I wait until morning, the flooding might make it impossible."

As much as she wanted to argue, she knew he was right. They had limited supplies here, and her father needed medicine beyond the herbs Reuben had on hand.

"How long will you be gone?" she asked.

"An hour. Two at most." He was already pulling on his coat, still damp from their earlier journey. "Keep the fire going. I brought in more wood. It's stacked behind that shelf." He pointed to a tall bookcase at the far end of the room.

Her father stirred at the sound of their voices. *"Warte,"* he called weakly. "Wait, Reuben."

Reuben paused by the door, looking back at the bishop.

"We should…pray before you go," her father managed, though the effort of speaking clearly exhausted him. His breath came in shallow gasps, his face contorting with the strain.

"*Datt*, save your strength," Nan urged.

Her father shook his head slightly. "Too…important," he insisted, his voice barely audible.

Reuben hesitated by the door, his hand on the latch. Then, to Nan's surprise, he returned and knelt beside her father.

"You're right, Bishop," he said quietly. "But perhaps Nan should pray. You need to conserve your strength."

Her father nodded, his eyes drifting closed again.

Nan took a deep breath and bowed her head. *"Vater unser im Himmel,"* Our Father, who art in heaven, she began. "We ask for Your protection over Reuben as he ventures out into the storm. Guide his steps and bring him safely back to us. We ask for Your healing hand upon my *datt.* We thank You for providing this shelter in our time of need. And we trust You have provided the same for our family and our dear friends. We commit them all to your safekeeping. *Amen.*"

When she opened her eyes, she found Reuben watching her, an intensity in his gaze that made her heart beat faster. For a moment, something unspoken passed between them—gratitude, perhaps, or understanding.

"I'll return as soon as I can," he said, rising to his feet. "If anything changes with your father, there's a medical book on the second shelf from the bottom, third case from the left. It might help."

She nodded, committing the location to memory. "Be careful."

With a final glance at them both, Reuben pulled open the heavy door. A gust of wind and rain swirled in before he stepped out into the darkness, pulling the door firmly shut behind him.

The sudden silence felt oppressive. Nan added another log to the fire, then checked her father once more. The tea seemed to have had some effect. His breathing, while still labored, had settled into a steadier rhythm, and his face appeared more peaceful in sleep.

Satisfied that he was as comfortable as possible, Nan glanced around the library. Now that she was alone, curiosity stirred within her. What secrets did this place hold? What did these books reveal about the man who collected them?

She resisted, somewhat successfully, the urge to pry. But as she looked for something to read to keep herself awake while waiting for Reuben's return, she couldn't help but wonder what treasures of knowledge surrounded her.

Moving quietly so as not to disturb her father, Nan stood and approached the nearest bookshelf. Her fingers trailed lightly over the spines, reading titles by the flickering firelight. Farming almanacs, historical texts about the Shenandoah Valley, botanical guides and medical references lined the shelves in neat rows.

One section caught her attention—a collection of leather-bound journals and what appeared to be maps rolled and tied with twine. She selected one of the maps and carefully unfurled it on a small table.

It was a detailed rendering of Promise, their mountain ridge and the surrounding valleys, with careful notations about water courses, elevations and—most intriguing—flood lines marked in different colors, each dated. Some of the dates went back over a century.

Next to the map lay an open journal, the handwriting neat and precise. The page opened to where Reuben had recorded daily weather patterns, comparing them to historical records from decades past.

She stared at the meticulous notes, understanding dawning. This was why Reuben had been talking to her *datt* and the other bishops at the wedding. He hadn't been merely worried about the weather—he'd been studying patterns, predicting this very flood.

Before she could investigate further, the sound of the door latch caught her attention. She hastily moved back to her father's side just as the door swung open.

Reuben stood silhouetted against the night, rain dripping from his coat, his expression grim. He'd returned much sooner than expected—and from the look on his face, his mission had not been successful.

The door closed behind Reuben with a solid thunk. Water streamed from his coat and pooled at his feet as he stood just inside the threshold, taking in the scene before him. Nan knelt by her father's side, her face a mask of concern poorly hidden.

"The path to my cabin is gone," he said simply, answering her unspoken question. "A new stream has cut through it. The water's moving too fast to tread across it safely in the dark."

He didn't mention how close he'd come to trying anyway—how he'd stood at the edge of the churning water, calculating the risks before reluctantly turning back. The memory of the bishop trapped beneath the buggy had been too fresh and the thought of Nan facing a similar fate if he didn't return too haunting, so he fought his way back against a wind so strong he'd been knocked to his knees more than once on the way.

"Will we be able to reach it in the morning?" Nan asked, her voice steady despite the concern in her eyes.

"Perhaps," he replied, though he wasn't as hopeful as he tried to sound. "If the rain stops completely overnight." He glanced at the windows, where water still streamed down the glass. The pounding of rain on the roof had lessened, but the wind still howled like a ferocious beast. The storm was far from over.

He shrugged off his sodden coat and hung it on a peg near the door, then bent to remove his boots. The simple action felt strange with Nan watching. This space had been his alone for so long that even these basic motions felt oddly intimate with an audience.

"How is he?" Reuben asked, nodding toward the bishop.

"Sleeping now," Nan replied. "The tea helped, I think. And the binding."

Reuben moved to the fire, holding his chilled hands toward the flames. The warmth barely penetrated his cold skin. "Good. Rest is what he needs most right now."

His eyes scanned the library, mentally cataloging their supplies. The food he kept here was minimal—enough for himself when he spent long days reading, not for three people potentially stranded for days. The water in his rain barrels outside would be plentiful after this downpour, but retrieving it would be challenging in the storm. Firewood would last perhaps two days, longer if the daytime temperatures continued to be as warm as they had been recently. Medical supplies were basic at best.

"We'll need to be careful with our resources," he said, turning back to Nan.

She nodded, her face solemn in the flickering light. "I understand."

A flash of lightning illuminated the stained glass window, casting brief jeweled colors across the room before plunging them back into the amber glow of firelight. Thunder followed seconds later, a deep rumble that seemed to shake the very foundation of the library.

Reuben moved to the window and peered out. In the brief flash of another lightning strike, he caught a glimpse of the fear in Nan's eyes. A chill ran through him that had nothing to do with his wet clothes.

Just like before, he thought. The images superimposed themselves in his mind—Lancaster, years ago, water rising around the dairy barn, animals trapped inside, his cousin's face as he realized what was happening…

"Reuben?"

Nan's voice cut through the memory. He turned to find her watching him, a furrow between her brows.

"Are you *oll recht*?" she asked. "You're shivering."

He hadn't noticed, but she was right. "Just need to dry off," he said, moving away from the window.

From a chest near his sleeping area, he retrieved a dry shirt and trousers. "I'll change behind the shelves," he said, a hint of awkwardness in his voice. Even with the bishop asleep and Nan's attention focused on her father, the library suddenly felt too small for the privacy he was accustomed to.

When he returned, dressed in dry clothes, Nan had settled on the floor beside her father, her back against a shelf of books, her legs tucked beneath her skirt. She looked exhausted, dark circles forming beneath her eyes.

"You should rest," he told her, gathering a blanket from his chest. "I'll keep watch over your father."

She shook her head. "I'm not tired," she insisted, though her drooping eyelids betrayed her.

"Nan," he said, his voice unusually gentle, "you won't help him by exhausting yourself."

For a moment he thought she would argue—that familiar stubborn set to her jaw appearing—but then her shoulders slumped slightly. "Wake me if anything changes?"

"I promise."

She adjusted her position, leaning more fully against the bookshelf, but didn't lie down. Her eyes remained on her father's sleeping form, her gaze protective.

Reuben settled into his chair at the far side of the fire, positioned so he could see both Nan and her father. Outside, the storm continued its assault, wind howling around the stone chimney, rain beating against the windows.

This library had always been his refuge from the world, a place where he could retreat from judgment and painful memories. Now it sheltered not only him but also the two people whose opinions had once mattered most to him in Promise: the bishop who had welcomed him despite the whispers that followed him from Lancaster, and the bishop's daughter who had never quite trusted his solitary ways.

His gaze lingered on Nan. She fought sleep valiantly, her head nodding forward only to jerk upright again, her eyes blinking rapidly before drooping once more. In the firelight, her profile was softened, the determined set of her mouth relaxed in exhaustion. Her prayer earlier had surprised him—not that she would pray, but the simple, direct way she'd spoken to God, so sure He would answer.

It reminded him of his mother's prayers, of a faith he'd once embraced without question before doubt and guilt had crept in to erode its foundations.

The bishop stirred, a soft moan escaping his lips. Reuben was beside him instantly, checking his pulse, feeling his forehead for signs of fever. The skin was warm but not alarmingly so—yet. He adjusted the binding around the bishop's chest, careful not to wake him.

"Is he worse?" Nan asked, leaning toward him.

"No change," he assured her. "Just dreaming, perhaps."

She nodded, relief evident in her features, then stifled a yawn.

"Sleep, Nan," he urged again. "I'll wake you if needed."

This time she didn't argue. Her eyes closed, her breathing gradually deepening as exhaustion finally claimed her. In sleep, the wariness she usually wore around him disappeared, replaced by a vulnerability that made something twist in Reuben's chest.

Outside, the wind changed direction, sending a new onslaught of rain against the windows. Reuben moved silently to check that no water was seeping in. The old stone structure remained solid, though a slight dampness on the sill beneath one window suggested he might have a leak after all, if the rain continued much longer.

As he turned back to the fire, his eye caught on the section of shelves where he kept his father's journals and the maps they'd been studying together before the bishop's accident. Had Nan been looking at them? The map of the mountain wasn't as he'd left it.

The thought didn't anger him as it might have once. Instead, he felt a strange relief. Perhaps it was time for some of his secrets to come to light—not all at once, but gradually, like dawn breaking over the mountain.

He returned to his chair, settling in for the long night ahead. The bishop's breathing had steadied somewhat, though it still carried a concerning rattle. Nan slept soundly, her head tilted at an angle that would surely leave her neck aching by morning.

Careful to move as silently as possible, Reuben took his spare blanket and draped it over her. She stirred slightly but didn't wake, her body instinctively curling into the warmth.

He returned to his vigil, watching over them both as the storm raged on and the night deepened toward its darkest hour.

Nan woke with a start, disoriented by the unfamiliar surroundings. For a moment, she couldn't remember where she was—then the events of the day came rushing back. The storm. Her father's accident. Reuben's library.

The fire had died down to glowing embers, casting just enough light to make out shapes in the darkness. Her father still lay by the hearth, his chest rising and falling in a shallow rhythm. Across from her, Reuben's chair sat empty.

A blanket slid from her shoulders. She didn't remember covering herself. Reuben must have placed it over her while she slept.

The thought stirred something warm and comforting within her. She pushed it aside, focusing instead on easing the stiffness in her neck from sleeping against the bookshelf. As she stretched, she caught sight of a figure silhouetted against one of the windows—Reuben, standing motionless as he gazed out into the night.

Careful not to disturb her father, Nan rose and made her way across the room. The floorboards creaked beneath her feet, alerting Reuben to her approach. He turned, his expression hidden in shadow.

"You should be sleeping," he said, his voice a low rumble in the quiet room.

"I did," she replied, coming to stand beside him at the window. "How long was I asleep?"

"A few hours. It's just past midnight."

Outside, the rain continued, though it had softened to a steady patter rather than the driving torrent of earlier, and the wind came in bursts rather than the nonstop battering that had seemed may never end. Still, through the streaked glass, she could make out vague shapes of trees bending in the wind.

"Has the water risen?" she asked.

"Some. Not as much as I feared. And we seem safe from any flowing water here." He glanced down at her. "Your father's breathing easier. The binding seems to have helped."

"I believe it has." She eased closer to Reuben and spoke quietly so as not to wake her *datt*. "Thanks to you."

He shrugged, seemingly uncomfortable with her gratitude. "Anyone would have done the same."

"No," she contradicted firmly. "Not anyone could have freed him from beneath that buggy. Not anyone would have known how to splint his leg or bind his ribs. Not anyone would have had this place—" she gestured around them "—this *sanctuary* to bring us to."

He didn't respond immediately, his gaze returning to the window. When he finally spoke, his voice was softer than she'd ever heard it.

"The shirt I used for your father's binding belonged to my *datt*."

"I'm sorry," she said automatically. "If I'd known—"

"No," he cut her off. "It was the right thing to do. My *datt* would have been the first to insist on it." A smile touched his lips, visible in the faint light from the dying fire. "He was the most generous man I've ever known. The most principled."

She'd never heard Reuben speak of his family before. The revelation that he'd had a father he clearly admired deeply opened a door she hadn't even known existed.

"What was he like?" she asked softly.

Reuben was silent for so long she thought he wouldn't answer. Then, as if a dam had broken, words began to flow.

"He built the dairy farm from nothing," he said, pride evident in his voice. "Started with just four cows and a small plot of land. By the time I was sixteen, we had over a hundred head and supplied milk to three counties." He shook his head, lost in memory. "He worked from sunrise to sunset, every day. Never complained."

"He sounds remarkable," Nan said.

"He was." Reuben's hands gripped the windowsill. "When he died—it was sudden, his heart—I tried to fill his shoes. Thought I could do even better than he had. Modernize. Expand." His voice turned bitter. "Pride comes before a fall."

Nan heard the defeat in his voice, saw it in the slump of his shoulders. This was the burden he'd carried all these years, she realized. The weight that had kept him apart from others, isolated in his grief and shame.

"What happened?" she asked gently.

Outside, a gust of wind rattled the windowpanes. Reuben's reflection wavered in the glass.

"Another time, perhaps," he said, his voice closing off again. "You should rest more. Dawn's still hours away."

She wanted to ask more questions while he seemed willing to talk, but the shuttered look had returned to his face. The moment of openness had passed.

"I'll check on *Datt* first," she said, stepping away from the window.

Her father slept soundly, his face peaceful in the dim light. The binding around his chest had loosened slightly; she carefully readjusted it, taking comfort in the steady, if labored, breathing.

Beside her, Reuben was stoking the fire, adding small pieces of wood to build it back up. The growing flames illuminated his profile—the strong line of his jaw beneath his beard, the furrow between his brows that never seemed to fully smooth out.

"You should sleep, too," she said, returning to where her blanket lay on the floor. "I can keep watch for a while."

He shook his head. "I'm used to long nights. Reading." He gestured to the books surrounding them.

As she settled back against the bookshelf, arranging the blanket around herself, a thought occurred to her. "Those journals and maps," she asked, pointing to the shelf. "Where did you get them?"

His hands stilled momentarily in the act of arranging the logs. "They were passed down through my family," he spoke reverently. "Others are mine. I've kept records like my *datt* taught me."

"That's how you knew about the flooding risk. You weren't just guessing or being cautious. You saw the pattern."

He nodded, his focus returning to the fire. "I saw what happened before. What happens when you ignore the signs." His voice dropped so low she barely caught his next words. "What happens when you think you know better."

There was so much more to ask, but something in his expression kept her silent. Whatever secrets Reuben carried, whatever failures haunted him, he carried them deeply. She couldn't pry them loose in a single night, no matter how the unusual circumstances had momentarily lowered his defenses.

As she was learning to do with Reuben, Nan held back her instinct to question relentlessly, allowing silence to fill the space between them.

Reuben moved away from the fire, returning with something folded over his arm—another blanket, this one a patchwork quilt of faded blues and greens.

"This will be warmer than what you have," he said, holding it out to her.

She took it, her fingers brushing his in the exchange. The quilt was soft with age and use, clearly handmade with care. Another piece of his past, she realized, offered without explanation.

"Denki," she said, spreading it over herself. It carried a faint scent of cedar and something else—lavender, of course, making her wonder what condition his fields would be in after this.

"Sleep well, Nan," he said, returning to his chair.

As she settled into the quilt's warmth, Nan found herself wondering about the hands that had sewn it. His *mamm*? *Grossmammi?* A sweetheart he'd never mentioned? The mystery of Reuben Bender seemed to deepen with each small revelation.

Her eyes grew heavy again, the rhythm of the rain on the roof lulling her to sleep. The last thing she saw before drifting off was Reuben's silhouette against the firelight, steady and watchful, his presence oddly comforting in this strange night of storms and secrets.

What other treasures and sorrows did this library hold? What other parts of Reuben's past were shelved among these books, waiting to be discovered? Tomorrow might bring answers—or more questions.

For now, wrapped in a quilt from his past, watched over by a man she was beginning to see with new eyes, Nan surrendered to sleep.

Chapter Eight

Nan awoke to a gentle warmth on her face. Golden light streamed through the stained glass window, casting jewel-toned patterns across the wooden floor.

She was still wrapped in the patchwork quilt Reuben had given her. The fire in the stone hearth burned steadily, evidence that he had tended it throughout the night while she slept. Her father lay nearby on a makeshift bed of blankets, his chest rising and falling in the shallow rhythm that had become familiar.

Reuben was awake and kneeling beside her father, resting the back of his hand against her *datt*'s forehead. He glanced up when he heard her move.

"He's not too feverish," he said quietly. "And the rain has finally stopped."

Nan pushed back the quilt and moved to her father's side.

"*Denki* for watching over him," she said. "Will you sleep now?"

Reuben shook his head. "I'm used to long nights." He stood, towering over her as he always did, but somehow the intimidating effect had lessened after their midnight conversation. "I need to try to reach my farm today."

"Is that safe, yet?" Her heart quickened with concern.

"Daylight makes it possible to see the dangers," he explained. "I need to check on my animals, and we need supplies." His gaze moved to the window. "The storm has passed for now, but the water will continue to rise. We need to use this break."

Nan nodded, thankful he was ready with a plan but fully aware of the exhaustion evident by the dark circles under his eyes. "When will you sleep?"

"After we have food, for one thing." A hint of a smile touched his lips. "And I need to retrieve my chain saw. I couldn't see well last night, but I saw enough to know there will be fallen trees blocking any path we might take to get your *datt* to help. I need to clear a way."

The practicality of his thinking reassured her. Here was a man with a plan—not just waiting for rescue, but actively working toward it.

"How long will you be gone?" she asked.

"Hard to say." He moved to the window, peering out at the transformed landscape. "The damage looks extensive. But I'll return as quickly as I can."

Her father stirred, a soft moan escaping his lips. Both Nan and Reuben were at his side in an instant.

"*Datt?* Can you hear me?" Nan took his hand, relief flooding through her when his fingers closed around hers.

His eyes fluttered open, awareness returning slowly. *"Nan,"* he whispered. "Where…?"

"We're safe," she assured him. "In Reuben's…library." She hesitated on the word, still unsure how her father would react to this obviously worldly collection of books.

"*Ya*, I remember now." To her surprise, her father's gaze moved around the room, taking in the shelves with no sign of judgment. His eyes settled on Reuben. "You're going out?"

Reuben nodded. "To get supplies. And to clear a path so we can get you proper help."

Her father raised a trembling hand and motioned to Reuben. *"Kumm."*

Reuben hesitated, then knelt beside him again. Her father's

hand moved to rest on Reuben's head, the gesture unmistakably one of blessing.

"Der Herr schütze dich," he whispered. "May the Lord protect you."

Something shifted in Reuben's expression—a softening Nan had rarely seen before the trials of the past twenty-four hours. He bowed his head briefly under the bishop's touch.

"Denki," he said simply when he looked up again.

The moment held a sacred quality that moved Nan deeply. Her father, even in his weakened state, remained a spiritual shepherd. And Reuben, for all his solitary ways, had accepted that blessing with humility.

As Reuben rose and began gathering his few supplies, Nan was struck by a sudden impulse. She reached into the pocket of her apron and withdrew a small folded paper—a verse her father had given her years ago, which she always carried in times of trouble.

"Take this," she said, holding it out to Reuben. "Somehow I sensed to bring it with me to the bakery yesterday morning." Just yesterday—a day that felt like a month.

He hesitated, then accepted the paper, his large fingers careful as he unfolded it.

"'Ich vermag alles durch den, der mich stark macht, Christus,'" he read aloud. "I can do all things through Christ which strengtheneth me."

For a moment, their eyes met, and Nan felt a connection beyond words—an understanding that transcended their differences and the brief time they'd known each other. In this crisis, something had changed between them.

"I'll keep it safe," he promised, carefully tucking the paper into his shirt pocket, as though he carried her finest treasure. Perhaps he did. "There's water in that jug, and wood enough for the day. If your father's pain worsens, there are more herbs in the small box by the hearth."

She nodded, aware of his hesitance to leave them. "We'll be fine. Just…come back safely."

He paused at the door, looking back at her with an expression she couldn't quite read. "I will."

The door closed behind him, leaving Nan alone with her father in the quiet library. Outside, she heard Reuben's mule snort and the sound of hoofbeats gradually fading into the distance.

"He's a *goot* man," her father said softly from behind her.

Nan turned, surprised to find him watching her with clear eyes. "You should rest, *Datt*."

"Misunderstood," he continued as if she hadn't spoken. "But *goot*."

She settled beside him, adjusting the blankets. "I'm beginning to see that."

Her father's eyes drifted closed again, but a faint smile remained on his lips. "*Gott* works in mysterious ways," he murmured before sleep reclaimed him.

Nan sat back on her heels, considering her father's words. She'd never imagined being trapped in Reuben Bender's secret library during a hurricane and flood, dependent on his help, discovering aspects of his character she'd never suspected existed.

Gott worked in mysterious ways, indeed.

Through the stained glass window, sunlight continued to stream, painting the library in colors that made the strange situation feel less threatening. Whatever lay ahead, they had shelter, they had hope, and help would be on the way.

For now, that would have to be enough.

Reuben guided his mule carefully between fallen trees and debris, mindful of hidden hazards beneath the mud and standing water. The familiar path to his farm was barely recognizable. Where there had once been a clear trail, there was now a maze of downed branches, uprooted underbrush and newly formed rivulets carving channels through the soil.

The devastation was worse than he had imagined. Even with his years of studying weather patterns and dreading this very scenario, the power of this storm staggered him.

It could take him days to make a path clear enough to bring the bishop through.

Reuben's hand unconsciously moved to his shirt pocket where Nan's verse rested. *I need your help, Gott. We need your help.*

"Easy, Solomon," he murmured as the mule hesitated at a particularly deep puddle. The animal had served him faithfully for years, possessing the sure-footedness and stubborn determination that made mules ideal for mountain terrain. Today, those qualities might mean the difference between success and failure.

As they crested a small rise, Reuben's farm came into view. Relief washed through him at the sight of his cabin and barn still standing. The structures appeared intact, though surrounded by fallen trees and scattered debris. His lavender fields—what remained of them after the fire—were now partially submerged, barely visible above muddy water in the lowest sections.

The sight of them reminded him of Nan and her determination to rescue what he'd deemed a lost cause. He wouldn't underestimate her again, not after this.

He urged Solomon forward, picking their way down the slope toward the clearing. Already his mind cataloged what needed to be done. Check the animals, gather food and supplies, retrieve the chain saw from the workshop, assess the most direct route back to the library that could be cleared for moving the bishop.

The weight of responsibility pressed on him. Despite the rumors that had followed him from Lancaster, the bishop had welcomed him to Promise. Naaman had defended him when others questioned. And then, he'd blessed Reuben this morning with trembling hands that nonetheless conveyed absolute faith.

And Nan…

The memory of her blue eyes watching him leave, concern

evident in their depths, stirred something he'd long kept dormant. For years, he'd maintained his distance from the community, convincing himself it was better that way. Safer. Less chance of failure or disappointment—for himself and for others.

But in a crisis, walls crumbled. Necessities overcame preferences. And maybe, just maybe, connections formed that couldn't so easily be severed once the emergency passed.

A movement at the edge of his clearing caught his attention, pulling him from his thoughts. Solomon's ears pricked forward, detecting the disturbance before Reuben fully processed what he was seeing.

People. Emerging from the woods on the far side of his property.

Reuben tensed, automatically scanning for signs of danger. Four figures moved slowly toward his cabin—a man, a woman and two children. Not Amish, judging by their clothing.

As they drew closer, he didn't recognize them as local neighbors, either. He could see their exhausted state. The man supported the woman, who limped heavily. The older child—a boy in his early teens—carried a large waterproof case clutched protectively to his chest. The younger child, a small girl perhaps seven or eight, trailed behind, her face streaked with dirt and tears.

Reuben urged Solomon forward, making his presence known. The family froze at his approach, wariness evident in their postures.

"Do you need help?" Reuben called, keeping his voice calm and unthreatening.

The man straightened, visibly gathering strength. "Our vacation cabin was destroyed in the storm. Our SUV washed away, too," he replied. "We've been walking for hours trying to find help."

Reuben dismounted as he reached the family, who must be tourists renting a cabin for the fall foliage season. Up close, their condition was even more concerning. The woman's ankle was swollen to twice its normal size. The children's faces showed signs of exposure and exhaustion.

"I'm Reuben Bender," he said. "This is my farm."

"James Elliott," the man replied, extending his hand after a moment's hesitation. "My wife, Sarah, our son, Michael, and daughter, Emma."

Reuben shook the offered hand, feeling the calluses that spoke of a man accustomed to physical work. "You're welcome to shelter in my cabin."

Relief flooded the man's face. "Thank you. Sarah needs to get off her feet. We think her ankle might be broken. We have a few supplies," James added quickly, as if afraid Reuben might rescind his offer if they seemed to be a burden. "And I have a ham radio. It's a hobby of mine. Brought it for fun, or so I thought. Instead, I've been trying to reach emergency services all morning. So far my connections have been spotty."

Reuben's attention sharpened. "A radio?" He glanced at the waterproof case the boy still clutched. "You can communicate with the outside?"

James nodded. "When I can find the right frequency. Cell towers are down, but radio operators are coordinating rescue efforts. I thought if I could find a clearing, we'd have a better chance."

For the first time since discovering the bishop's accident, Reuben felt a spark of real hope. This unexpected encounter might be the answer to their most pressing problem—getting medical help for the bishop.

"I have someone injured, as well," Reuben said. "Naaman Burkholder, our bishop. He's trapped at a shelter not far from here with his daughter. He needs medical attention."

James's expression grew serious. "How badly is he hurt?"

"Broken leg. Possible broken ribs or a punctured lung. He's having trouble breathing."

Sarah spoke up, her voice strained but determined. "That sounds serious. James can try to contact emergency services once we get a good radio connection."

Reuben nodded his thanks, then gestured toward his cabin. "Let's get you settled first. Then I need to feed my animals and gather supplies to take back."

He led the way, supporting Sarah on one side while James took the other. The children followed, the girl's small hand reaching up to pet Solomon's nose as they walked.

"Your horse is big," she said, the first words she'd spoken.

"He's a mule," Reuben corrected gently. "Stubborn but reliable."

"Like my dad," she replied with such innocent certainty that Reuben couldn't help but smile slightly.

At the cabin, Reuben helped settle Sarah on his small couch while James immediately began unpacking the radio equipment. Michael hovered close to his father, watching intently as components were arranged on the table.

"I need to check my animals," Reuben explained. "Make yourselves at home. There's a pump for water outside if you need it. Probably should boil anything before drinking. The well is deep but could be contaminated."

James nodded his thanks, already focused on connecting wires and adjusting dials. The practiced movements spoke of experience—not a casual hobby but a skill regularly maintained.

Outside again, Reuben headed for the barn. His three goats bleated their displeasure at being confined during the storm. He checked them quickly, providing fresh water from the rain barrel and feed. The chickens were similarly unharmed but unhappy, clucking indignantly as he scattered grain in their coop.

As he worked, his mind raced with revised plans. The radio changed everything. If they could contact emergency services, perhaps help could come to them rather than them struggling to transport the bishop over treacherous terrain.

Still, he couldn't count on immediate rescue. He needed to prepare as if they would have to move the bishop themselves. After securing the animals, he went to his workshop where the chain saw was stored.

When he returned to the cabin, James was speaking into the radio microphone, his voice clear and professional.

"KG4RTF calling emergency coordination net, reporting survivors and medical emergency in Promise area, over."

Static crackled, then a voice responded: "KG4RTF, this is W4VEM at Henry County Emergency Management. Go ahead with your report."

Reuben stood silently, listening as James provided their location and described both Sarah's injury and the more serious condition of the bishop. The methodical exchange of information and the calm professionalism of both speakers conveyed competence that reminded Reuben of his father's approach to farming—no wasted words, no unnecessary emotion, just clear communication of essential facts.

"We have reports of extensive flooding in your area," the radio operator replied. "Ground access is currently impossible. We're coordinating helicopter evacuations for medical emergencies. What's your exact location?"

James looked to Reuben, who stepped forward. "We're due west of Promise almost exactly three-quarters of a mile, as the crow flies. But the bishop isn't here. He's still trapped at a location in the woods."

James relayed this information, then listened to the response. "They need coordinates or a landmark visible from the air," he told Reuben.

Reuben thought quickly. "My lavender fields. They're visible from above. The library where the bishop is located is about a quarter mile north beyond the fields, in the woods."

James repeated this information into the radio, then listened again. His expression grew serious as he turned back to Reuben.

"They say a medical evacuation helicopter might be able to reach us late this afternoon if weather holds. But they can't land in woods. We'd need to move the bishop to the lavender fields before dark."

Reuben nodded, already calculating what that would require. "I'll need to clear a path. I can't do it alone before nightfall."

"Michael and I will do all we can to help." James spoke with a determination that reminded Reuben of his little girl's reference to being as stubborn as a mule, and Reuben knew *Gott* had answered his prayer for help.

Sarah spoke up from the couch. "James, tell them about the conditions further south. What we heard before."

James nodded grimly, turning back to the radio. After another exchange, he set down the microphone and looked at Reuben.

"It's much worse than we realized. The western North Carolina mountains took the brunt of the storm. Multiple communities cut off. Dams threatening to breach. They're prioritizing resources there, which means help here will be limited."

The weight of this information settled on Reuben. This wasn't just a localized emergency affecting a few families. This was a regional disaster that would strain every available resource.

"Then we must do all we can to help each other," he said firmly. "My home is here for you, and any food you need is yours." He looked at Sarah. "And you need to rest. I have an old crutch in the shed to fetch for you."

Young Emma, who had been sitting quietly in a corner, suddenly spoke up. "Are we going to help the bishop, too?"

Reuben looked at the child, her innocent question cutting through the complexity of the situation to its essence. *"Ya,"* he answered before remembering to use English. "Yes, we are."

James stood. "What do you need us to do?"

"I need to gather food and supplies. Load up Solomon." Reuben glanced at the chain saw he'd retrieved. "Then I need to start clearing a path back to where the bishop and his daughter are sheltering."

"Michael and I can help," James offered. "Once I've made sure Sarah and Emma are comfortable."

Reuben nodded his acceptance, surprised by how naturally this partnership had formed. These strangers—*Englischers,* no less—had become partners in the span of minutes.

As he began gathering supplies, Reuben's thoughts returned to Nan waiting anxiously at the library, and to her father whose life might depend on their success. The verse in his pocket seemed to weigh more heavily now, a reminder of strength beyond his own.

I can do all things through Christ which strengtheneth me.

For the first time in years, Reuben allowed himself to truly believe those words might apply to him.

Chapter Nine

The hours stretched endlessly as Nan kept vigil beside her father. She'd made him as comfortable as possible with the limited resources at hand—adjusting his makeshift pillow, offering sips of water, rewetting the cloth on his forehead when fever threatened. His breathing remained labored but stable, each rise and fall of his chest a reassurance that he continued to fight.

"Datt," she whispered, though he slept on, unresponsive. "You must get well. There are so many who need you."

Her words dissolved into the silence of the library. She hadn't realized until this moment how much she had always taken her father's steady presence for granted. The bishop of Promise was a fixed point around which their community revolved—offering counsel, mediating disputes, guiding them all with gentle wisdom. Watching his life hanging in the balance shook her deeply.

And the wondering about everyone else was increasing her anxiety as she paced the library floor. Her family? Cassie and Martin? Everyone she knew and loved had to have been in some form of danger last night. How had they fared? When would she know?

Unable to stand the endless questions racing through her thoughts and helpless to find any answers, Nan found her gaze drawn to the shelves surrounding her for a diversion. With daylight streaming through the windows, she could see the full extent of Reuben's collection. Books of every size lined the walls, neatly organized but abundant enough to suggest years of careful collecting.

Surely, simply exploring the books wouldn't be too nosy.

She rose quietly and approached the nearest shelf. Agricultural texts, botanical references, historical accounts of the Shenandoah Valley—all arranged by subject and author. Her fingers skimmed their spines, pausing occasionally to pull one out and leaf through it.

Moving along the shelf, she came to a section that seemed more personal. Leather-bound journals stood in a neat row, their spines marked with years. The oldest dated back to the 1950s—long before Reuben's time. She carefully pulled one from the shelf, opening it to find pages filled with detailed weather observations, crop yields and predictions for the coming seasons. At the bottom of each entry was a signature: *Abraham Bender*.

"His grandfather?" she murmured to herself, replacing that volume and selecting one from the 1980s. The handwriting had changed, but the meticulous attention to detail remained the same. This one was signed *Jacob Bender*—Reuben's father, she presumed.

The newest journals were clearly Reuben's own, continuing the family tradition of painstaking recordkeeping. She noticed that the most recent volume had extensive notes comparing current conditions to those recorded by his father and grandfather decades earlier.

He saw the patterns. He knew what was coming because he was afraid of history repeating itself.

The realization struck her forcefully. Reuben's warnings to her father and the other bishops had come from years of preparation. This whole time he'd been devoted to careful and detailed study.

As someone with a knack for noticing minute details and piecing them together to understand the people and happenings around her, she suddenly realized that she and Reuben weren't so different.

People thought she was merely curious or nosy, but that wasn't the whole of it. She knew, though she rarely dwelt upon it, that she found a sense of security in knowing and understanding what was happening around her. She noticed things to protect herself.

But what had driven Reuben to such lengths? Who or what was he trying so hard to protect?

Setting the journal back in its place, Nan moved deeper into the library. Behind a row of books on local history, she discovered a folder of correspondence—letters between Reuben and other Amish communities about weather patterns and warnings. Some responses were dismissive, others grateful. Scattered among them were newspaper clippings about floods and storms dating back decades.

One letter in particular caught her attention. From a bishop in Ohio, it thanked Reuben for his warning that had allowed their community to move livestock to higher ground before a flash flood. *Others called your predictions alarmist,* the bishop had written, *but the six feet of water that swept through our lower pastures proved you right. You saved many animals and livelihoods through your diligence.*

Next to the folder lay a small wooden box. Nan hesitated, knowing this was crossing further into Reuben's private domain. But something about it drew her hand forward. Inside were photographs—a younger Reuben standing proudly beside an older man in front of a large dairy barn, a family gathered around a dinner table, a farmhouse surrounded by fields.

Lancaster. His life before Promise.

Did the photos mean they'd allowed a journalist to write a story about their farm?

Another compartment of the box held pressed lavender, the dried blooms still fragrant even after months or years preserved between sheets of paper. And beneath them, a half-finished carving of a lavender stem, the wood smooth from handling, the detail exquisite even in its incomplete state.

"*Ach*, Reuben," she whispered, carefully returning everything to the box. "You are more than you let anyone see."

The image of Reuben that was forming in her mind differed so greatly from the aloof, taciturn man she thought she knew. Here was evidence of a man deeply connected to his family's past, committed to helping others through his knowledge, possessing an artistic sensitivity she never would have guessed at.

"Nan."

Her father's voice startled her. She quickly closed the box and returned to his side.

"*Ya*, *Datt?* I'm here." She took his hand, noticing with relief that his eyes seemed clearer than before.

"Water?" he requested.

She helped him take a few sips, supporting his head. "How do you feel?"

"Like I've been stepped on by a horse," he replied, his attempt at humor ending in a grimace of pain. "Reuben?"

"Gone to his farm for supplies," she explained. "He should return soon."

Her father's eyes traveled around the library, taking in the shelves of books. "Quite a collection."

"*Ya,*" she agreed hesitantly, still uncertain how he would react to the revelation of this library.

To her surprise, a faint smile touched his lips. "Always learning, always preparing." His voice grew fainter with the effort of speaking. "A *goot* man. Blessed to have him among us."

"Rest, *Datt*," she urged, seeing exhaustion creeping over him again. "Save your strength."

He nodded slightly, his eyes drifting closed. "*Gott* brings people into our lives for a reason, Nan," he murmured. "Remember that."

Her father's breathing deepened into sleep once more, and Nan sat back on her heels, pondering his words.

A sudden loud crack from outside startled her from her thoughts. She rose quickly, moving to the window. Another sharp report—the sound of wood splitting—echoed through the forest. A tree falling?

Her heart raced, knowing she couldn't move her *datt* from danger again. Not alone.

She strained to see through the trees, but the dense growth obscured her view. As she listened, the sporadic cracking continued, then gradually transformed into a different sound—a mechanical buzzing that rose and fell in pitch.

A chain saw.

Relief flooded through her. Reuben had returned, and he was already working to clear a path. The steady drone of the saw continued, growing closer with each passing minute.

"He came back, *Datt*," she said, though her father couldn't hear her. "Just as he promised."

The comfort of that surprised her in its intensity. In the hours since Reuben had left, she'd found herself worrying about his safety, wondering if he'd encountered obstacles too great to overcome. The whine of the chain saw dispelled those fears, replacing them with a new certainty.

Whatever challenges lay ahead, they wouldn't face them alone.

She moved about the library, preparing for Reuben's return—gathering the few items they might need to transport, ensuring her father was ready to be moved when the time came. The mechanical buzz continued outside, interspersed with shouts that suggested Reuben wasn't working alone.

Had he found others from their community? The thought both relieved and concerned her. Relief that more help might be available, concern about what conditions others might have endured during the storm.

The chain saw fell silent, but voices carried on the still air. Reuben's deep baritone was joined by others—a man's voice, a boy's higher pitch, even a child's gleeful call.

The sound of multiple people approaching through the woods filled Nan with mingled curiosity and caution. Who had Reuben found? What news did they bring of the world beyond these walls?

As the voices drew nearer, Nan smoothed her apron and adjusted her *kapp*, suddenly aware of her disheveled appearance after more than a day in the same clothes. She moved to the door, pausing with her hand on the latch.

Whatever came next—whatever challenges awaited them—she would meet them with the strength she'd discovered in herself during these hours alone. And with the surprising comfort of knowing Reuben Bender was a man who kept his promises.

The last fallen tree blocking the path to the library finally surrendered to Reuben's chain saw, its massive trunk sectioned into manageable pieces that he and Michael dragged to the side of the trail. Sweat soaked his shirt despite the cool air, muscles burning from hours of continuous labor.

"That should do it," he said, shutting off the saw. The sudden silence felt almost physical after the machine's constant drone.

James wiped his brow, leaning against a tree trunk. "You think we can get a stretcher through now?"

"Ya," Reuben confirmed, surveying their work. The path wasn't wide, but it was passable—clear enough to transport the bishop safely if they were careful. "We're almost there. The library is just beyond that rise."

Young Emma, who had insisted on coming along despite her parents' concerns, peered ahead eagerly. "Is it a real library? With storybooks?"

Reuben glanced down at the child, still surprised by how easily she had overcome her initial shyness around him. "It's my private collection," he explained. "But *ya*, there are some storybooks."

Her face brightened. "Can I read them while the grown-ups talk?"

The question caught him off guard. His library had never been a place for children—had never been a place for anyone but himself until yesterday. Yet now he found himself nodding. "If your father says it's alright."

Michael shouldered the makeshift stretcher they had constructed from wooden planks and blankets from Reuben's cabin. "Dad, should I scout the path?"

James shook his head. "We stay together. Safety in numbers."

Reuben approved of the man's caution. In the few hours they'd worked together, he'd come to respect James Elliott's practical nature and methodical approach. Despite being an *Englischer*, the man shared many values Reuben had been raised to hold dear—hard work, careful planning, putting family first.

They gathered their tools and supplies, then continued along the freshly cleared path toward the library. Reuben led the way, increasingly aware of his own eagerness to return. The concern for the bishop's condition was paramount, of course. But there was also Nan—waiting, watching, perhaps wondering if he would keep his promise to return.

The verse she had given him remained in his pocket, a tangible connection to her even as he'd worked. He found himself touching it occasionally throughout the day, drawing strength from the words and from the knowledge that she had entrusted it to him.

As they approached the final bend in the path, Reuben paused, turning to the others. "The bishop's daughter, Nan, doesn't know I've brought company. Let me go ahead and explain."

James nodded his understanding. "We'll wait here."

Reuben continued alone, emerging from the trees into the

small clearing before the library. The stone and timber structure stood unchanged, a testament to its builders' skill centuries ago and his own careful restoration. Smoke curled from the chimney, a sign that Nan had maintained the fire as he'd instructed.

Nan stood waiting for him by the opened door, her blue eyes wide with relief. "*Denki Gott* you're safe," she said, the words rushing out. Then, noticing his appearance, she said, "*Ach*, you're filthy."

The unexpected observation—so unfiltered, so *Nan*—drew a rare smile from him. "*Ya*. Chain saw work is messy." He glanced past her to where the bishop lay. "How is he?"

"The same." She stepped back, allowing him to enter. "I heard the saw. You've cleared a path?"

Reuben nodded, removing his hat. "And I've brought help."

"*Ya*, I heard the voices. Who?"

"A family whose rental cabin was destroyed in the storm. They have a ham radio—a way to contact emergency services." He saw hope flare in her eyes and continued quickly. "The Elliotts—James, Sarah and their children. Sarah's injured her ankle, so she remained at my cabin, but James and the children came to help."

"Englischers?" The question held no judgment, only curiosity.

"*Ya*. Good people. The radio is important, Nan. They've already contacted rescue services. A helicopter might come later today for your *datt*—if we can get him to the lavender fields before dark."

The implications settled over her features—relief, hope, determination. "Then we must hurry."

"I'll bring them in. James has been coordinating with emergency services all morning. He'll explain everything."

She nodded, smoothing her apron nervously. Reuben turned to wave the others forward. As the Elliott family approached, he found himself watching Nan's reaction—her initial surprise giving way to a warm welcome as she ushered them inside.

"Naaman Burkholder," she introduced, gesturing to her father who had awakened at the sound of new voices. "Bishop of our district."

James approached respectfully, introducing himself and his children. Michael remained quiet, but Emma immediately moved to the shelves, her eyes wide at the sight of so many books.

"Your daughter is welcome to look at the books," Reuben told James, seeing the man's concern at Emma's curiosity. "There are some illustrated volumes on the lower shelves that might interest her."

While the child happily explored, James removed the portable radio from his pack and explained what they had learned about the situation beyond their immediate area.

"The flooding is widespread," he told them, setting up the radio on a small table. "Roads are washed out. Bridges down. The National Guard has been mobilized, but they're focused on the areas hardest hit in North Carolina."

Nan's face paled. "How bad is it?"

James's expression turned grim. "Worse than anything in recent memory. Multiple communities isolated. Dams at risk of failing." He adjusted a dial on the radio, which emitted soft static. "Emergency services are stretched thin, but they've prioritized medical evacuations. And many private helicopter pilots are volunteering their help for rescues, as well. When I described your father's condition, they agreed to try to send a medical helicopter."

"Thank you." Gratitude nearly overwhelmed her, leaving her lost for more words.

James continued, "They can't land in these woods, though. We need to transport the bishop to an open area visible from the air."

"The lavender fields," Reuben confirmed. He turned to Nan. "The path is clear now, but moving your father will still be difficult."

The bishop spoke up, weak but determined to stand. "I can manage."

"*Datt*, no," Nan protested. "You cannot bear weight on that leg."

Reuben gestured to the stretcher Michael had brought in. "The Elliotts helped me construct a new stretcher at my cabin, since the one from last night took a beating getting here. And we have pain medicine from my cabin," Reuben added. "It might help make the journey more bearable."

The radio suddenly crackled to life. "KG4RTF, this is Henry County Emergency Management. Do you copy?"

James quickly moved to the device. "This is KG4RTF. I copy."

"We have a medical evacuation helicopter scheduled for your location at approximately seventeen hundred hours. Weather system moving in from the west may force earlier arrival. Can you confirm patient will be at the designated extraction point?"

James looked to Reuben, who nodded firmly.

"Affirmative," James replied. "We'll have the patient at the extraction point within two hours."

"Copy that. Stand by for further instructions."

As James continued the exchange with emergency services, Reuben moved to where Nan stood watching, her face a mixture of hope and concern.

"It will work," he said quietly, just for her ears. "Your *datt* is strong."

"I know," she replied, though uncertainty lingered in her eyes. "But he's so frail right now…"

"We'll be careful," he assured her. "And we have help."

She looked up at him, studying his face with an intensity that might once have made him uncomfortable. Now, he found himself meeting her gaze steadily, willing her to see his determination.

"You found the Elliotts when they needed help," she observed softly. "Just as you found us when we needed it."

He shook his head slightly. "Perhaps *Gott* arranged these meetings, not me."

A small smile touched her lips. "Perhaps."

Young Emma approached, clutching a book she'd discovered. "Mr. Reuben, is this yours?" She held up an illustrated volume of Bible stories that had been tucked among more scholarly texts.

Reuben nodded, surprised she had found it and still unused to being called mister. "My mother used to read those stories to me when I was your age."

"Could I borrow it?" Her hopeful expression was difficult to resist. "I'll be very careful."

Before Reuben could respond, Nan answered for him. "I'm sure Reuben wouldn't mind, but we must leave here very soon."

Emma looked momentarily disappointed but accepted the answer with a nod. "Okay. Dad says we might need to hurry because of the helicopter."

"That's right." Reuben knelt down to Emma's level. "But you may take this book with you, if you like."

Reuben's heart clenched at the warmth in the child's eyes. "Oh, thank you, Mr. Reuben."

He patted Emma on the head as he stood, only to catch Nan's approving smile, which melted his heart more than he'd known possible. Invigorated by her approval, he immediately moved into action, organizing their limited belongings. "We should take only what's essential. I'll return for the rest later."

As they prepared, Reuben found himself working in seamless coordination with Nan. Without words, they anticipated each other's needs—she gathering blankets to keep her father warm, he tinkering with the stretcher for extra stability, she securing the bishop's Bible in her apron pocket, he checking the bindings to ensure they would hold during transport.

This unspoken understanding between them felt both new and somehow familiar, as if they'd always had this capacity for harmony but had never before had cause to discover it.

When everything was ready, they carefully moved the bishop onto the stretcher. Despite their gentleness, the transition clearly caused him pain. Nan knelt beside him, murmuring encouragement.

"We'll go slowly," Reuben assured him. "The path is clear, but still rough in places."

The bishop nodded, his lined face set with determination. "*Gott* will provide strength."

James instructed Michael on how to help carry the stretcher, positioning Reuben at the front and himself at the back, with Michael supporting one side. "Nan, could you watch Emma and carry the radio?" he asked.

She nodded, accepting the portable device and taking the young girl's hand. Emma looked up at her with immediate trust, and Reuben noticed how naturally Nan assumed this caretaking role.

As they prepared to leave the library, Reuben paused at the threshold. This place had been his sanctuary, his private refuge for years. Now it had served as a shelter for others in crisis, and he realized there'd be no going back to how things were before this storm.

"Ready?" James asked from behind him.

Reuben nodded, stepping outside. "*Ya.* Let's go."

The small procession moved carefully through the forest, following the path Reuben and James had cleared earlier. The bishop remained stoic despite the inevitable jostling, his eyes fixed on the canopy of leaves above them, lips moving in what Reuben assumed was silent prayer.

Nan walked beside the stretcher, occasionally touching her

father's hand in reassurance. Emma stayed close to her side, asking occasional questions in a whispered voice that Nan answered patiently.

As they neared the edge of the woods where the lavender fields began, Reuben felt a curious mixture of emotions. Pride in his property—even damaged by flood—mingled with apprehension about what lay ahead. The rescue, the bishop's recovery, and life once the crisis passed.

The more they learned about the damage from the storm, the less likely it seemed that anything would ever be the same again. And would things between him and Nan go back to how they'd always been? That possibility troubled him more than he cared to admit.

They emerged from the tree line into the late afternoon sunlight. Before them stretched Reuben's lavender fields, subdued by mud and water in the lower sections but still visible enough to serve as a beacon from above. The higher ground at the field's edge remained relatively dry—a perfect landing spot for the helicopter.

"This is it," Reuben announced, carefully lowering his end of the stretcher in the center of the clearing. "The driest and most level ground on the property."

James nodded in approval, then turned to the radio to confirm their position. Nan helped make her father as comfortable as possible while they waited, adjusting blankets and offering water.

She turned to him, something unspoken in her expression. "*Denki*, Reuben. For everything."

Before he could respond, the radio crackled with new information. James listened intently, then looked up with relief clear on his face.

"The helicopter is en route," he announced. "ETA fifteen minutes."

Reuben watched as Nan's hand found her father's, their fingers intertwining in a gesture of shared hope. The bishop's eyes met his across the clearing, a quiet acknowledgment passing between them.

Whatever came next, they had reached this moment together—bishop, daughter, reclusive neighbor and *Englisch* strangers—united by crisis into an uncommon closeness.

As the distant sound of rotor blades began to echo across the valley, Reuben found himself hoping that some part of that unity might remain when the waters receded and life in Promise made its way back to a new normal.

His gaze returned to Nan, finding her already watching him, her blue eyes reflecting the same unspoken question that echoed in his own heart.

What happens after the storm?

Chapter Ten

Standing at the edge of Reuben's lavender fields, Nan kept her eyes fixed on the sky. The storm had passed, leaving behind an unbelievable calm. Brilliant blue stretched overhead with only a few wispy clouds, as if denying the destruction that lay all around them. The air smelled fresh—washed clean of the previous day's heaviness.

"How much longer?" young Emma asked her father, who stood nearby with the radio pressed to his ear.

"Not much longer," he replied. "But this will be the last flight today. Nightfall's coming."

Nan's gaze dropped to her father on the makeshift stretcher, his eyes closed as he conserved his strength.

"Datt?" She knelt beside him. "The helicopter will be here soon."

His eyes flickered open. *"Goot,"* he whispered. "Promise is blessed to have such help. *Gott* will bring us all through."

Nan smiled to comfort him, though worry continued to gnaw at her. They'd heard nothing yet about conditions at her *grossmammi*'s farm. Were they all safe? The farmhouse was high on a hill, likely protected from flooding. But the wind…*ach* but the wind had been relentless.

She offered up a silent prayer for them all—*Grossmammi*, *Tante* Lena, Rose and both boys, Daniel and Tommy.

She glanced toward Reuben, who stood several paces away,

scanning the horizon. The set of his shoulders revealed his tension, though his face remained calm for the benefit of the others. He'd been like this since they emerged from the woods onto his property—vigilant, focused, as if personally responsible for the helicopter's arrival.

Something new had happened between them during their time in the library. She'd glimpsed the man behind the gruff exterior—a man of knowledge, foresight and unexpected gentleness. A man who kept his promises, even when they were difficult to fulfill.

Emma tugged at her skirt, breaking into Nan's thoughts. "Will the helicopter be very loud?"

"I imagine it will," Nan replied, giving the hand a gentle squeeze. "But don't be afraid. It's bringing help for my *datt*."

"Michael says they have big propellers that make wind," Emma continued. "Will they blow us away?"

She'd never been anywhere near a helicopter, either, but despite her own worry, Nan tried to reassure the *kinner*. "We'll stand well back when it lands. Your father will tell us where it's safe."

The girl nodded solemnly, clearly processing this information with great seriousness. "Mr. Reuben said as long as we don't get too close, we won't get blown over. He said it won't be as bad as the wind last night, and it will be over soon enough."

"Did he now?" Nan glanced again at Reuben, who had moved to stand beside her father. The thought of him explaining helicopters to an *Englisch* child was curious. He did seem to know an awful lot about some things most Amish didn't—like helicopters, for one. But the thought of him carefully explaining it so comfortingly to a scared child also warmed something inside of her.

James's voice rose with sudden urgency. "I hear it! Everyone get ready!"

Nan strained her ears, then caught it—a distant thudding

that grew steadily louder. Reuben was immediately in motion, directing Michael and James on how to position the stretcher, gesturing for Nan and Emma to move back.

"Stay behind that rise," he instructed, pointing to a slight elevation at the field's edge. "The downdraft can be dangerous."

Nan guided Emma to the indicated spot, then hesitated. "My *datt*—"

"We'll handle him," Reuben assured her, his voice firm but kind. "Keep Emma safe."

The thudding noise intensified until it seemed to fill the entire valley. A dark shape appeared over the tree line, growing larger as it approached. Wind whipped around them even before the helicopter was directly overhead, its powerful rotors bending the remaining lavender stalks in waves, like purple water rippling in a pond.

Nan pulled Emma close, shielding the child with her body as flying debris swirled around them. Through squinted eyes, she watched as the helicopter descended into the center of the clearing. Men in bright safety vests jumped out while the rotors continued to spin, rushing toward where her father lay with Reuben, James and Michael standing guard against the artificial windstorm.

Everything happened with dizzying speed after that. The emergency crew assessed her father, transferred him to a proper stretcher and prepared him for transport. One of them approached her, shouting to be heard above the noise.

"We can take one family member! Are you coming?"

The question struck her unprepared. Of course she should go with her *datt*. He needed her. And yet—her gaze moved to Emma clinging to her skirt, to Sarah who couldn't walk properly, to Reuben who stood watching her with an unreadable expression.

Before she could answer, her father's voice called out with surprising strength. "Nan stays! Others need her help here!"

The medic looked at her questioningly. Nan hesitated, torn between her duty to her father and her responsibility to those remaining behind.

"What about Sarah? She should go and have her ankle looked at." Nan couldn't go and leave the injured woman here.

James shook his head. "I already tried to convince her. She won't leave without us."

"It's your choice," Reuben said, suddenly beside her. "I promised the bishop we'd get to your family as soon as we can to help them. I will do all I can, even if you must go."

When they got to them, not *if.* The quiet confidence in his voice steadied her. And she believed he would do all he could in her absence.

The medic was growing impatient. "We need to decide now. Daylight's fading."

Nan knelt quickly beside her father as they prepared to load him into the helicopter. *"Datt—"*

His weathered hand found hers. "Be strong, *dochder.* I will be in *goot* hands. Others need you, and Reuben needs you."

Something in his eyes—a knowing look she couldn't fully interpret—caught her attention. Before she could ask what he meant, he squeezed her hand once more, then let go.

The medics lifted his stretcher, carrying him efficiently toward the waiting helicopter. Nan stood frozen, watching as they secured him inside. One of the crew gave a thumbs-up signal, and the door slid closed.

The engines roared louder as the helicopter prepared to lift off. Reuben's hand came to rest lightly on her shoulder—barely there, yet somehow anchoring. The gesture surprised her, but she didn't pull away. Instead, she found herself leaning slightly toward him as the helicopter rose into the air, carrying her father away to safety.

They stood together, watching until the aircraft was merely

a dark speck against the brilliant post-storm sky. Only when it had disappeared completely did Nan realize she was trembling.

"He will be well cared for," Reuben said softly.

She turned to face him, suddenly aware of how close they stood, unable to find words to express all her heart felt in that moment.

"Denki," was all she could manage.

His amber eyes held hers for a heartbeat longer than necessary. *"Gern geschehen."* You're welcome, came his gentle reply.

The moment stretched between them, something unspoken passing in the space of a breath. Then Emma tugged at Nan's dress, breaking the connection.

"Is your papa going to be okay?" the child asked.

Nan smiled, pushing aside the complicated emotions Reuben's nearness had stirred. "Yes, the doctors will help him now."

James approached, the radio in his hand. "They've confirmed your father's been approved for a bed at the hospital. The doctors will treat him as soon as possible after his arrival."

Relief washed through her, releasing the tightness in her chest. "Praise *Gott*," she whispered.

"We should head back to the cabin before it gets too dark," Reuben said, scanning the horizon where the sun was beginning its descent. "We can prepare for the night. The cabin is small, but there's room enough for the women in the cabin and men in the barn."

Nan nodded, grateful Reuben's cabin was merely yards away, plainly visible at the edge of the clearing. The previous night's journey through the woods to his hidden library had been so harrowing that this basic convenience was a *wunderbar* relief.

"If we keep trying," James added, "we might establish better radio contact tonight. See if we can get news of your family."

"I have a solar battery backup. We can use it to keep your radio charged," Reuben said quietly, fatigue beginning to show in his tone but his steady determination still evident.

As they gathered their few belongings, Nan found herself walking beside Reuben. "I didn't thank you properly," she said. "For everything you've done."

He glanced down at her, his expression softening in a way she'd rarely seen before the events of the past couple days. "I made a promise to Bishop Vernon Mast to help if a storm came," he said simply.

"Is that the only reason?" The question slipped out before she could stop it.

Reuben's pace slowed as he considered her words. *"Nay,"* he said, his gaze meeting hers with a depth of sentiment that took her breath. "It's not."

He didn't elaborate, and Nan didn't press, but a door between them that had previously been firmly shut was slowly opening up.

Reuben watched as Nan, insisting Sarah rest her injured leg, prepared a simple supper from the supplies he'd gathered before the helicopter arrived. The cabin's main room felt crowded with so many people, yet somehow not uncomfortable. Light from oil lamps cast a warm glow over the scene as darkness fell outside.

He'd never imagined his small home filled this way—with voices, movement, life. For five years, he'd maintained his solitude, convincing himself it was what he preferred. Now, watching Nan laugh at something Emma said, he wondered if he'd been lying to himself all along.

James worked at the table, fine-tuning the radio that had so far failed to connect with anyone who might have news of Nan's family. The frustration was evident on his face, mirroring what Reuben felt inside. Surely Jake would be trying to reach Promise by now, concerned for his nephews. But then, Reuben couldn't be sure his cousin had gotten news of the storm. Or how devastating it had been here.

"Any luck?" Reuben asked, approaching the table.

James shook his head. "Atmospheric conditions aren't ideal." He adjusted a dial, producing only static. "I'll keep trying."

"Denki," Reuben said simply.

"Your cousin Jake," James began, "the one who helped design your barn—you mentioned he's married to Nan's sister?"

"*Ya*. Aubrey, the bishop's eldest daughter. They were away when the storm hit." Reuben's concern deepened as he spoke. Jake would be frantic about the boys. "They have custody of Jake's two nephews—Tommy and Daniel. My kin, too. The boys stayed with Nan's family while Jake and Aubrey went on their honeymoon."

James nodded understanding. "I'll keep trying to get information. Emergency services are coordinating search and rescue across the affected areas. And that sounds more and more like a very large area. Damage is even worse further south of here, though it's hard to imagine. Apparently, we didn't see the worst of it locally."

Reuben wasn't sure if that was good or bad. Certainly, he hated to think of others having it worse than what he'd witnessed so far. But for the Burkholders that might be a very good thing.

"The Burkholder farm sits higher than most," Reuben offered, hoping this fact provided some comfort to Nan, who he knew was listening while pretending not to. "And the house is solid. Built solid by Amish workmen."

Nan approached, wiping her hands on her apron. "Supper is ready," she announced, though her smile didn't quite reach her eyes.

They gathered around the table—an unusual assembly of Amish and *Englisch* sharing a meal in the aftermath of disaster. Michael helped Sarah to her place while Emma insisted on sitting beside Nan. Reuben found himself at the head of his own table, a position that suddenly felt weightier than before.

"Would you like to say grace?" he asked James, uncertain of their customs.

The man looked momentarily surprised, then nodded and bowed his head. "Lord, we thank You for Your protection through the storm, for the food before us and for bringing us together in this time of need. Watch over those still missing, heal those who are hurt, and guide those working to help others. Amen."

"Amen," Reuben and Nan echoed together.

The simple meal of bread, dried meat and preserved vegetables felt like a feast after the tension of the day. Conversation flowed more easily than Reuben would have expected, with Emma's innocent questions drawing smiles even from Michael, who had remained mostly silent until now.

"Where will everyone sleep?" the girl asked, looking around the small cabin.

Reuben had been considering this question himself. "The women and children can have the cabin," he said. "James and Michael and I will sleep in the barn."

"Is it a nice barn?" Emma asked seriously.

Reuben found himself smiling. "It is. My cousin Jake helped design it after the fire last summer. Built to withstand high winds."

"The community came together for a barn raising," Nan explained to the Elliotts. "That's our way when someone needs help."

"Like how everyone's helping each other now," Emma observed.

"Exactly like that," Nan agreed, her gaze meeting Reuben's across the table.

Something warm unfurled in his chest at the connection. Had anyone ever looked at him with such open appreciation before? Without judgment or expectation? He couldn't remember.

After the meal, they settled into evening routines. James

continued his efforts with the radio while Sarah told stories to Emma. Michael helped Reuben prepare the barn, carrying blankets and arranging sleeping areas in the clean, sweet-smelling hay of the loft.

Returning to the cabin, Reuben found Nan alone on the small porch, staring at the night sky. Stars filled the heavens in breathtaking clarity, the storm having washed away any haze that might have obscured them.

"May I join you?" he asked.

She nodded, making room on the bench. "It's so peaceful now," she said quietly. "Hard to believe what happened yesterday."

"Nature has a way of reminding us of our place," Reuben replied, settling beside her. "Both its fury and its beauty."

They sat in comfortable silence for a moment, the night sounds of insects and distant frogs filling the space between them.

"I found your family journals," Nan admitted suddenly. "In the library, while you were gone. I shouldn't have pried, but—"

"It's *oll recht*," he interrupted gently. "I'm not angry."

Her surprise was evident even in the dim light. "You're not?"

"Nay." He looked up at the stars rather than at her. "Perhaps it was time someone knew."

"Three generations of weather observations," she said with something like wonder in her voice. "That's how you knew the storm was coming."

Reuben nodded. "My *grossdawdi* began recording patterns after nearly losing everything in a flood. My *datt* continued and then taught me. When I saw the signs matching what happened before—" He trailed off, the weight of his family's past and his own failures pressing down again.

"You tried to warn everyone," Nan finished for him. "That's why you were speaking to all the bishops at Aubrey's wedding."

"Ya." He hesitated, then decided to offer the truth. "Not everyone believed me. Some thought I was being alarmist."

"But my *datt* listened."

"He did," Reuben agreed. "He always has."

Nan turned to face him more fully. "I misjudged you, Reuben. For years, I thought your reclusiveness was about pride or disliking people. But it wasn't that at all, was it?"

The directness of her question caught him off guard. In the soft glow spilling from the cabin windows, her blue eyes seemed to see straight through the walls he'd built around himself.

"In a way it was about pride. My pride that led to the need to come to Promise to start over," he said carefully. "After… after things went wrong in Lancaster."

"The dairy farm," she supplied. "I saw the photographs."

He nodded, something tight loosening in his chest at her simple acknowledgment. "I thought I knew better than generations before me. Modernized too quickly. When the equipment failed—" He stopped, the memory still raw even after years. "Lives were changed. Not just mine."

Nan's hand came to rest lightly on his arm. "But you're using that knowledge—your past, your family's past—now to help others."

"Too little, too late," he murmured.

"I don't believe that," she said firmly. "And neither does my *datt*. Why else would he tell me to stay here? He sees something in you worth trusting."

Her faith in him was both balm and burden. He didn't deserve it, yet found himself desperately wanting to.

"I can do all things through Christ which strengtheneth me." He withdrew the small folded paper she'd given him before he left for his farm. "It helped—" he held it out to return to her "—when the path seemed impossible to clear."

Instead of retrieving the paper, she pressed it back into his palm, her fingers warm against his. "Keep it," she said softly. "I think you need it more than I do right now."

He closed his hand around both the paper and, briefly, her fingers.

They fell silent again, but the quality of the silence had changed. No longer just comfortable, it now held possibility—as vast and shimmering as the starlit sky above them.

"I should get inside," Nan said eventually. "It's been a long day."

Reuben nodded, rising with her. "I'll check on James and Michael in the barn."

At the cabin door, she paused. "Reuben?"

"Ya?"

"You kept your promise," she said simply. "To come back."

Before he could respond, she had slipped inside, leaving him standing in the starlight with her words echoing in his mind and the small paper clutched in his hand like a lifeline.

You kept your promise.

Such a simple observation, yet it struck him with unexpected force. For years, he'd lived with the weight of what he perceived as his greatest failure—a promise to his family in Lancaster that he couldn't fulfill. Perhaps, in Nan's eyes at least, he was beginning to redeem that broken trust.

As he walked toward the barn where James and Michael waited, Reuben found himself looking back at the cabin. Through the window, he could see Nan helping Sarah prepare for bed, her movements gentle yet efficient. The sight stirred something long dormant within him—a yearning for relationship he'd denied for too long.

The storm had passed, leaving destruction in its wake. But it had also cleared away some of the barriers he'd so carefully constructed around his heart. What would grow in their place remained to be seen.

One thing was certain. Nothing between him and Nan Burkholder would ever be quite the same again.

Chapter Eleven

Dawn painted the eastern sky in delicate pinks and golds as Nan slipped from the cabin into the crisp morning air. Sleep had eluded her for most of the night, her mind refusing to quiet despite her exhaustion. Every time she closed her eyes, images of the storm's destruction flashed behind her eyelids, quickly followed by worried thoughts of her family.

Had *Grossmammi* Esther's farmhouse withstood the winds? Was Rose safe? And what of the two young boys, Tommy and Daniel, who must be so frightened without their Uncle Jake?

She pulled her shawl tighter around her shoulders, her breath forming small clouds in the cool air. The sun was just beginning to peek over the ridge, illuminating a landscape transformed by the storm. The previous day's blue skies remained, as if nature was apologizing for its fury by offering perfect clarity to survey the damage.

A soft crackle of static drew her attention to the cabin's small porch, where James Elliott sat hunched over his radio equipment. He'd arranged it on a small table Reuben had carried out for him, the various components connected by a tangle of wires leading to what James had called a solar battery.

"You're up early," she said softly, approaching him.

James looked up, his face showing signs of his own sleepless night. "Atmospheric conditions are sometimes better at dawn," he explained. "I thought I'd try again to get clear communication."

"Any luck?" The question caught in her throat, hope and fear tangled together.

"Not yet, but—" He stopped as the radio suddenly emitted a clearer burst of sound. "Wait, I think…" His fingers moved quickly across the dials, fine-tuning until a voice emerged through the static.

"KG4RTF, this is Augusta County Emergency Management. Do you copy?"

James's face lit up as he grabbed the microphone. "This is KG4RTF. I copy you clearly. Over."

"What's your status? Over."

"We are located three-quarters of a mile west of Promise. Status is stable. Six individuals at our location—three adults, two minors, one with ankle injury. Bishop Naaman Burkholder was evacuated by helicopter yesterday evening. Requesting information on conditions in Promise Mountain area, particularly the Burkholder farm. Over."

Static crackled, then the voice returned. "Roads remain impassable in most of the affected area. Multiple bridges down. Three major landslides reported. Rescue operations continue, but several communities remain isolated, including portions of Promise Mountain. Over."

Nan's heart sank. She pressed her fingertips against her lips, fighting to maintain composure.

James glanced at her, then leaned toward the microphone again. "Any information specifically on the Burkholder property? Also, are you familiar with the Mennonite Aid Society or Bishop Vernon Mast? The survivors here are concerned about family members. Over."

A pause, then, "Stand by."

The silence stretched uncomfortably. Nan paced the small porch, sending up silent prayers. Behind her, the cabin door opened, and Sarah emerged, leaning on a walking stick Reuben had fashioned for her the previous evening.

"Any news?" she asked quietly.

Nan shook her head, not trusting her voice.

The radio crackled again. "KG4RTF, this is Peter Stoltzfus with Augusta County Emergency Management. I'm Bishop Mast's son-in-law. He asked me to coordinate communications for the Promise Mountain area when I told him about the storm's impact. Over."

James and Nan exchanged surprised glances.

"This is James Elliott. Thank you for that information. Do you have any news about the Burkholder farm or its residents? Over."

"The Burkholder property is where the Mennonite Aid teams have chosen to set up base camp operations for the Promise area under Jake Brenneman's direction as soon as possible. Aerial observation shows the farmhouse and other buildings are still standing, but we've had no direct contact with residents as phone lines are down. However, Bishop Mast has been organizing Mennonite Aid Society volunteers since yesterday and they hope to reach the property by midday. Over."

Nan exhaled shakily. The house was standing. That was something.

No wonder Reuben and her father had wanted her to remain at the farmhouse. They knew it was safer. And they must also have foreseen that Jake and Vernon would make quick work to arrive there with help if needed.

Her heart trembled with a depth of gratitude she hadn't ever experienced.

"Additionally," the voice continued, "I can confirm that Jake and Aubrey Brenneman have been in contact with Bishop Mast. They're currently attempting to return to Promise but are facing significant travel obstacles. Over."

James spoke into the microphone. "That's very helpful information. Any word on the condition of Bishop Naaman Burkholder at the hospital? Over."

"I will do my best to get you an update as soon as possible. Over."

"One final question," James continued. "Can you maintain contact with this frequency and relay any estimates for evacuation for my family when available? Over."

"Affirmative. Bishop Mast has instructed me to prioritize communications for the area for the Mennonite Aid Society. I'll check in every two hours with updates. Over."

"Much appreciated. We'll stand by. This is KG4RTF, over and out."

As James set down the microphone, the sound of footsteps approached from the direction of the barn. Nan turned to see Reuben crossing the yard, his tall figure silhouetted against the morning light. She watched as his pace quickened upon seeing them gathered on the porch, his expression shifting from its usual reserve to open concern.

"News?" he asked simply as he reached them.

As Nan filled him in on all the details, something flickered across Reuben's face—relief mingled with determination. "Then I have to go."

"What do you mean?" Sarah asked, though Nan already understood.

"I promised the bishop," Reuben said, his gaze meeting Nan's. "That I would look after his family. I have to go, and the sooner the better."

"*We* will go," Nan corrected, emphasizing the "we" with quiet conviction.

For a moment, she thought Reuben might object, but instead, he simply nodded. "We'll need to prepare."

"The terrain will have changed. It could be unstable and dangerous," James warned. "Perhaps Nan should stay."

Reuben's gaze turned back to Nan, a war of decision raging behind his amber eyes.

She straightened her shoulders, prepared to do battle, but didn't have to when Reuben answered James instead. "*Our* journey won't be easy. But once we clear a path, we can also get help to Sarah and get you folks back home."

Sarah wiped a tear from her cheek, and James squeezed her shoulder, as they both thanked them in unison.

As the sun climbed higher in the sky, Nan felt a surge of hope rise within her. They had a plan now, a purpose. And somehow, standing there with Reuben's steady presence beside her, the fears that had plagued her through the night seemed less overwhelming.

"We'll get through this," Reuben said quietly, as if reading her thoughts.

Coming from anyone else, such words might have seemed empty reassurance. But from Reuben Bender, Nan realized, they made all the difference.

Reuben moved with purpose. The sun had fully risen now, casting long shadows across his property as he strode toward the barn. Their decision to go to the Burkholder farm had been made without debate—an understanding reached with barely a word exchanged between him and Nan. He couldn't ask her to stay behind. She needed to go as much as he did.

As he prepared to leave, his hands knew what to do even as his mind worried over the dangers. He'd already checked Solomon's hooves before breakfast, ensuring his faithful mule was sound for the trip. Now he needed to gather supplies, prepare Nan's horse and collect the tools they might need to clear their path.

Inside the barn, the familiar scents of hay and animals greeted him. Solomon stood in his stall, ears pricked forward as if sensing the coming adventure. In the stall beside him,

Buttercup—Nan's pale golden mare that James and Michael had brought over from his library yesterday—nickered softly.

"You'll need to keep Nan safe again today," Reuben told the horse as he approached with a brush. "Your work is almost done, and I'll set you up with a fine bucket of oats once we get to the Burkholders'." The animal's coat was already clean, but the rhythmic strokes helped order his thoughts.

He moved to the tack wall, selecting Nan's saddle. As he adjusted the girth, his thoughts turned to Nan. Her determination to reach her family was admirable, but he couldn't help worrying about the dangers they might face.

Reuben finished with Buttercup's saddle and moved to prepare Solomon. Once both animals were prepared, Reuben gathered the remaining supplies. The chain saw went into a specially designed carrier that attached to Solomon's saddle. Extra fuel, rope, a small medical kit and blankets followed, packed efficiently into saddlebags.

When he emerged from the barn leading both animals, Nan was waiting in the yard. Her golden hair was neatly pinned beneath her *kapp*. Despite the circumstances, she looked composed, ready for whatever challenges lay ahead.

"I have water," she said, holding up a large canteen. "And Sarah has packed food for us."

Reuben nodded, impressed by her foresight. "Good thinking."

Nan approached Buttercup, running a hand along the mare's neck. "Ready for another adventure, old friend?"

Reuben moved to Solomon, checking the chain saw's secure attachment one final time.

Reuben checked Solomon's girth one final time, then glanced at Nan. "Ready?"

She nodded, moving toward Buttercup. Without thinking, Reuben stepped closer and interlaced his fingers to create a step for her. "Allow me."

A flicker of surprise crossed her face, followed by a small smile that warmed something long neglected within him. She placed her hand on his shoulder for balance, her foot in his cupped hands. With a smooth motion, he boosted her up as she swung gracefully into the saddle.

Their eyes met briefly as she settled herself, a wordless exchange that contained more meaning than Reuben could decipher. Then she gathered the reins, all business once more.

Reuben mounted Solomon with practiced ease, though the weight of responsibility settled over him.

"God be with you," Sarah called as they turned their mounts toward the eastern edge of the property.

"And with you," Nan called back, the traditional farewell carrying extra weight in their current circumstances.

As they rode away from the cabin, Reuben glanced back once. The Elliott family stood watching their departure—James with his arm around Sarah, Michael standing tall beside them and little Emma waving vigorously. Somehow, these strangers had become something more. Not quite friends, perhaps, but connected by shared experience in a way he couldn't dismiss.

He turned forward again, focusing on the journey ahead. The devastation became more apparent as they left the yard, with broken tree limbs scattered across the fields and deep channels carved by runoff water. Solomon picked his way carefully through the debris, his sure-footedness one of the reasons Reuben preferred mules for mountain travel.

"The stream will be our first real challenge," he told Nan as they reached the edge of his property. "After that, we'll need to navigate the forest path. It's likely blocked in places."

"We'll find a way through," she replied, her voice steady with determination. "We have to."

Looking at her profile against the morning sky, Reuben was struck by the quiet courage she displayed. Not reckless bravado, but a steady resolve to do what needed doing, regardless of difficulty.

It was, he realized, not unlike his own approach to problems. Perhaps they weren't so different after all, for all their contrasting ways of moving through the world.

The thought provided unexpected comfort as they rode into the unknown landscape ahead, side by side in the brilliant morning light.

The touch of Reuben's hands lingered in Nan's memory as Buttercup carried her through the transformed landscape. That brief moment when he'd cupped his hands to help her mount had been unexpected—gentle yet strong, a simple courtesy that revealed much about the man. She'd placed her hand on his shoulder for balance and felt the solid steadiness beneath her palm, much like the steadfast reliability she was coming to recognize in him.

They rode side by side where the terrain allowed. The familiar countryside had become a stranger almost overnight. Where gentle slopes had once rolled toward the horizon, jagged tears now cut through the earth. Debris scattered across fields once lush with summer growth. The scent of wet soil and broken vegetation hung heavy in the air.

Above them, the drone of helicopter rotors punctuated the morning. Nan looked up to see three aircraft moving in different directions across the vast blue sky—rescue operations underway across the mountains. The sight brought both comfort and concern. How bad must the damage be if so many helicopters were needed?

"The high meadow should be just ahead," Reuben called back to her, raising his voice slightly to be heard over a particularly low-flying helicopter. "From there, we can see how the stream is running."

Nan nodded, guiding Buttercup around a fallen branch.

Though focused on their path, she couldn't help studying Reuben as he rode ahead. His broad shoulders set with determination, his posture revealing both alertness to their surroundings and ease with his mount. Solomon responded to the slightest pressure of Reuben's knees, their communication almost wordless—the result of years together.

They crested a small rise, and Nan gasped at the view before them. The high meadow, normally a gently sloping expanse of wildflowers and grasses, had been transformed. What looked like a new stream cut diagonally across it, water still flowing briskly through the fresh channel.

"The runoff created new waterways," Reuben explained, his face grim as he surveyed the damage. "We'll need to find a crossing."

He dismounted, leading Solomon closer to examine the flow. Nan followed suit, allowing her horse to stretch her neck for a few mouthfuls of grass that had survived the deluge.

"It's not too deep here," Reuben said after a moment, pointing to a narrower section. "The animals can cross safely if we lead them."

As Nan approached the edge, Reuben's hand appeared before her, offered without comment. She accepted it, grateful for the support as they navigated the slippery bank together.

The water swirled cold around her ankles, soaking the hem of her already tattered dress. Buttercup followed without hesitation, accustomed to creek crossings from years on the mountain. On the opposite bank, Nan wrung out her skirt as best she could while Reuben checked Solomon's load.

"The chain saw's dry," he confirmed, adjusting the carrier. "We'll likely need it soon."

As if his words had summoned the challenge, not far into the woods the path was blocked by a massive fallen oak. Its root system had been torn from the softened ground, creating a wall of earth and twisted wood across their route.

"No way around?" Nan asked, though she could see the answer herself. The terrain on either side was too steep or too densely grown to navigate with the horses.

Reuben shook his head. "We'll need to cut through." He secured Solomon to a nearby sapling, then removed the chain saw from its carrier. "Stay back with the horses. There will be dust and debris."

Nan led both animals to a safe distance, watching as Reuben assessed the fallen giant. He approached the task methodically, first removing smaller branches to access the main trunk, then starting the chain saw with a practiced pull. The machine roared to life, its harsh buzz becoming a familiar sound.

With efficient movements, Reuben began cutting through the thick trunk. Sawdust sprayed as the blade bit deep into the wood. The work took nearly half an hour, the sun climbing higher as Reuben created a passageway through the obstacle and switched off the chain saw.

"That should be wide enough," he said, wiping sweat from his brow despite the cool morning air. "The horses can step over what's left."

As Nan led Buttercup forward, she noticed Reuben watching the sky with a frown.

"What is it?" she asked.

"More helicopters than before."

She followed his gaze to see at least five aircraft visible now, including one that hovered low over a distant ridge. "Is that good or bad?"

"Both, I think. Good that help is available. Bad that so much is needed." He secured the chain saw and remounted Solomon. "We should continue. There will be more obstacles ahead."

They rode in companionable silence for a time, each lost in thought. The surrounding forest told the storm's story—broken branches, upturned saplings and occasional clearings where trees had stood just days before. Yet amid the destruction, Nan noticed signs of resilience, too—a deer and fawn bounding away at their approach, birds calling to one another overhead, wildflowers somehow standing tall despite the battering they'd endured.

"It's strange," she said eventually, "how changed everything is at once and yet there's life trying to go on."

Reuben glanced back at her, something softening in his expression. "Nature recovers. It always has."

"Is that what your family's journals show? Recovery after disasters?"

He nodded. "My *grossdawdi* recorded the flood of '72, then how the valley fields came back richer the following spring. My *datt* documented drought years followed by abundant harvests." His voice grew quieter. "It helps to remember that what looks like an ending often isn't."

"I wouldn't have taken you for such a deep thinker, Reuben Bender."

A hint of a smile touched his lips. "There's a lot of time for thinking when you spend most days alone."

"Too much time, perhaps," she ventured, then immediately wondered if she'd overstepped.

But Reuben didn't bristle as he once might have. Instead, he seemed to consider her words seriously. "Perhaps," he conceded after a moment. "Though solitude has its purposes, too."

"Like what?" she asked, genuinely curious about his perspective.

"Clarity, sometimes. Space to understand oneself without others' expectations clouding the view." He guided Solomon around a muddy section of the trail. "But I'm beginning to see there are things solitude cannot provide, as well."

"Such as?"

He hesitated, as if choosing his words carefully. "Balance, for one thing, a lack of perspective beyond your own point of view." Another pause. "It's also sorely lacking in…companionship."

The final word seemed to hang in the air between them, laden with meaning neither was quite ready to articulate. Nan felt her cheeks warm slightly and focused on adjusting her grip on Buttercup's reins.

"I worry about my family," she said, changing the subject to safer ground. "Especially *Grossmammi.* She's strong, but at her age…"

"Esther Burkholder survived a blizzard with two small children while your *grossdawdi* was stranded in town," Reuben said, surprising her with this knowledge of her family history. "Your *datt* has mentioned her resourcefulness more than once."

"You're right," Nan admitted, finding comfort in the reminder. "And Rose is with her, along with *Tante* Lena. They'll have managed somehow." She stroked Buttercup's mane absently. "The boys are what concern me most. They've already lost so much. This kind of disaster could bring back difficult memories."

Reuben's shoulders tensed slightly. Tommy and Daniel were his kin, and little Daniel was particularly fond of Reuben.

They rounded a bend in the trail to find their path blocked again, this time by a tangle of smaller trees washed up against a stone outcropping. Reuben dismounted with a sigh, reaching for the chain saw once more.

"Another delay," he said, frustration evident in his voice.

"We're already on my grandmother's property," Nan reminded him, scanning the sky. The sun indicated it was now past noon. "It's not much further to the farmhouse."

As Reuben prepared to clear the obstruction, a distant sound caught Nan's attention—not helicopter rotors this time, but something else. She cocked her head, listening.

"Do you hear that?" she asked.

Reuben paused, chain saw in hand but not yet started. "Water," he said after a moment. "Moving fast. The stream must be higher than I expected."

They left the horses secured and proceeded on foot toward the sound. It grew louder as they approached, transforming from a gentle burble to an ominous roar. When they reached the edge of the trees, Nan stopped short at the sight before them.

The small stream that normally flowed gently beneath a stone bridge had become a rushing torrent. The bridge itself—a sturdy structure that had stood for generations—remained intact, but the waters swirled dangerously around it, carrying debris that crashed against the stonework with alarming force.

"We can't cross that," Nan said, stating the obvious. "Not here. But I know where the spring that feeds this stream begins. It's just a ways up. We can go around."

They returned to the horses and worked together to clear the path enough to proceed. They climbed higher along the ridge. The going was slower, the path less defined, but eventually they emerged onto a rocky outcropping that provided a sweeping view of the valley below.

Nan drew in a sharp breath at the panorama of destruction visible from this height. From the ground, they'd seen individual instances of damage—a fallen tree here, a washed-out section there. But from above, the storm's full impact became apparent. New waterways cut silvery paths across the landscape. Entire sections of forest lay flattened, trees pointing in the same direction like fallen soldiers. In the distance, what had once been a small lake had swelled to three times its size, drowning the surrounding meadows and filling quickly with the downed trees being washed away by the streams that fed into it.

"It's worse than I imagined," she whispered.

Reuben nodded grimly. "It will take years for some areas to recover fully."

Despite the sobering view, Nan found her gaze drawn to a particular point on the horizon. There, set on the hillside, stood the familiar silhouette of her grandmother's farmhouse. From this distance, it appeared untouched, its sturdy form a beacon of hope amid the surrounding chaos.

"Look," she said, pointing. "The farmhouse. It really is still standing."

They continued their journey, the new route taking them higher along the ridge before gradually descending toward the house.

By midafternoon, as the sun began its westward descent, they crested a final rise that brought the Burkholder farm into clear view. The farmhouse stood solid on its hillside perch, though the surrounding fields showed signs of the storm's passing. The barn appeared intact, but a smaller outbuilding had lost part of its roof. The kitchen garden had been partially washed away, and debris littered the yard.

Most surprising, however, was the activity visible around the property. Several vehicles were parked near the barn. People moved purposefully across the yard, carrying tools and supplies. A group of men worked to repair the damaged outbuilding, while others cleared fallen branches from the lanes.

"The Mennonite Aid Society has arrived," Nan said, confusion giving way to dawning understanding. "Look at how many people are there. They must have arrived not long after our radio contact with Vernon's son-in-law."

Reuben's expression revealed similar surprise. "Vernon Mast is in charge for a reason. No grass grows under his feet."

Relief washed through Nan, bringing unexpected tears to her eyes. Her family was not alone. Help had arrived.

"Haw," she urged Buttercup forward with renewed energy. "We're almost there."

As they made their final approach to the farm, Nan found herself glancing at Reuben. The closer they got to the farm, the more his posture stiffened, his shoulders squaring as if preparing for battle rather than reunion.

During their journey—working together, talking, overcoming obstacles side by side—something had blossomed between them. A partnership that felt natural and right. For the first time, Nan had glimpsed what it might be like to truly know Reuben Bender, and to be known by him in return.

But now, watching his expression close like a book snapping shut, she felt a flicker of worry. Would he withdraw again once they rejoined the others?

Before she could voice her concerns, a small figure broke away from the group near the house, running toward them with unmistakable excitement.

"Nan! Reuben!"

Tommy's voice carried clearly across the yard, his legs pumping as he raced to meet them. Behind him, little Daniel followed, his younger face split with a welcoming grin.

Nan's heart lightened at the sight of the boys safe and sound. She dismounted, eager to reach them and wrap them in her arms. Beside her, Reuben straightened in his saddle, his expression momentarily softening at the children's approach before that guarded look returned.

Something in the way he scanned the gathered crowd told her all she needed to know. Among so many people—perhaps even those who had once judged him—Reuben was already considering his retreat once more into solitude, convinced it was where he belonged.

Their journey had ended. They had arrived. But Nan couldn't shake the feeling that another journey—the one between her heart and Reuben's—might be in danger of ending before it truly began.

Chapter Twelve

Reuben felt the change sweep through him like a building wave as they approached the Burkholder farm. The openness he'd found during their journey—that unexpected ease of conversation with Nan, the simple partnership they'd formed facing each obstacle—suddenly being swept away. In its place rose the familiar vigilance that had been his companion these past five years.

Too many people. Too many eyes watching, judging.

Tommy reached them first, his small body colliding with Solomon's side as he skidded to a stop. "Reuben! Aunt Nan! You came!"

Despite his growing unease, Reuben couldn't help the warmth that spread through him at the boy's excitement. He dismounted quickly, lifting Tommy into a brief embrace before setting him back on his feet.

"Of course we came," he said, his voice gruffer than he intended. "Are you alright? And Daniel?"

"We're fine," Tommy assured him, bouncing slightly on his toes. His animated expression dimmed only slightly as he added, "The cellar was scary, but Rose told us stories. And *Grossmammi* Esther said we were brave as David facing Goliath."

Daniel caught up then, moving at a more cautious pace but

with equal enthusiasm. "We helping." His eyes beamed as he pointed to the muddy evidence on his pants.

Nan gathered both boys into her arms, her relief palpable. Over their heads, her eyes met Reuben's, a question in their depths. She'd noticed his tension, then. Of course she had. Nan noticed everything.

He ought to reassure her. About what? That he wouldn't ignore the new thing growing between them. That he wouldn't forget how alive she made him feel. That he wouldn't return to his library alone when all of this was over.

But those feelings growing inside of him over the past few days had been swiftly uprooted the second Nan had urged her horse toward the farm. Toward reality—one suspended just long enough for him to lose sight of it and hope for something different.

But this farm bustling with volunteers and community working together with practiced efficiency—this was Nan's reality. And he'd almost forgotten that he didn't belong in it.

Nay, he wouldn't offer her promises he couldn't keep.

He looked away, scanning the busy farmyard instead. At least a dozen men worked to repair the damaged outbuilding, their coordinated movements suggesting experienced labor. Several women moved between house and yard, carrying supplies or directing smaller children in simple tasks. The well-organized activity spoke of leadership.

The familiar authoritative figure of Bishop Vernon Mast approached them, his weathered face creased with both concern and relief.

"*Willkumm*, Nan, Reuben," Vernon greeted them, extending his hand to Reuben first. "We've been praying for your safe arrival."

Reuben accepted the handshake, noting the strength in the older man's grip despite his years. "The path was challenging but doable," he reported. "How long have you been here?"

"A few hours now. The mountain roads were blocked or washed out in places requiring some detours, but we made it." Vernon looked around at the work surrounding them. "Our focus right now is to coordinate teams to reach the most isolated areas." His eyes showed genuine appreciation as he continued, "Your warning gave me crucial time to prepare, Reuben, even before the forecast changed. The Mennonite Aid Society had volunteers ready to deploy as soon as the wind and rain subsided."

Reuben shifted uncomfortably at the praise, but was thankful nonetheless to have been able to help.

Nan had released the boys and moved to join them, her face alight with questions. "My *grossmammi*, *Tante* Lena and Rose? They're well?"

"All safe," Vernon assured her. "Your grandmother showed remarkable presence of mind, moving everyone to the cellar before the worst winds hit. The house suffered minimal damage, though I can't say the same for the fields and the lake."

Reuben had noticed the devastation as they approached. A painful sight, knowing how Jake and Aubrey had worked to restore the fields after years of neglect.

"Not all is lost," Vernon added, noting their grim expressions. "The field nearer the house remained more protected by the ridge. The others will dry out and with some work can be productive again come spring."

A small comfort, Reuben thought, though better than none.

As Vernon led them toward the house, a slender young man emerged from the barn, carrying a toolbox. Reuben recognized Jake's other cousin Lukas, who had served as an attendant alongside him at the wedding. The young man's face brightened upon seeing them.

"*Dank sei Gott* you've made it safely," Lukas said, approaching. "We were so relieved to learn Nan and the bishop had been with you. But then, we weren't sure if the trails would be passable for you to get back here."

"Reuben cleared the way," Nan replied, an unmistakable note of confidence in her voice that made something twist uncomfortably in Reuben's chest. How long until he disappointed her?

But rather than dwell on the inevitable, he spoke to Lukas instead. "How have things been here?"

"Manageable," Lukas answered. "I was staying in Jake and Aubrey's cabin while they were away, helping with farm tasks. When the storm hit, I came to check on everyone here." His gaze drifted briefly toward the house, where a flash of red hair was visible through the window. "Rose was looking after the boys. We all sheltered together until it passed."

Reuben noticed the slight color that rose in the young man's cheeks at the mention of Nan's sister. Interesting. Quiet Rose and confident Lukas—perhaps there was a connection forming there.

"The Elliots?" Nan whispered in his ear. "Do they know about them?"

Not wanting to waste any time getting help to the family left back at his farm, Reuben pulled Vernon aside to fill him in on the situation. "And now that we've cleared a path, I'd like to get back to them as soon as possible. They are welcome to my home as long as needed, but the wife needs medical attention."

Vernon rested a comforting hand on Reuben's shoulder. "The Elliots will be our top priority. Private helicopters are on the move to help now, as well. I'll do what I can to coordinate with the authorities. Hopefully someone can get them out quickly."

The front door of the farmhouse opened, and Nan's *grossmammi* emerged, her lined face breaking into a wide smile at the sight of her granddaughter. Behind her stood Rose and elderly *Tante* Lena, both looking tired but unharmed.

"Praise be. *Kumm*," Esther called, opening her arms.

Nan rushed forward, embracing her grandmother with visible relief. "I was so worried," she admitted, her voice muffled against the older woman's shoulder.

"Psh," Esther dismissed the concern, though her tight grip betrayed her own relief. "The Burkholders have weathered storms before." She released Nan and, to Reuben's surprise, turned her warm gaze on him. "And here is the young man who helped bring our Nan home safely."

Uncertain how to respond to such an open welcome, Reuben merely nodded respectfully. "*Grossmammi* Esther. I'm glad to find you well."

"Come inside, both of you," she insisted. "You must be exhausted and hungry after such a journey."

Reuben glanced around at the ongoing work. "I should help with the repairs," he said, already looking for an escape from the intimate setting of the farmhouse.

Vernon shook his head. "Rest first. There will be plenty of work remaining tomorrow. And I'll take care of the Elliots." He gestured toward Reuben's distant farmland.

A sudden relief momentarily overshadowed Reuben's discomfort of being in such a large gathering. After all the intense worry of the past days, knowing those in his care were finally safe overwhelmed him to the brink of tears.

He drew in a shaky breath that no one seemed to notice.

Except Nan. Of course.

But her observant eyes and her caring nod reassured him. He was oddly thankful for her notice. Could get used to it even.

And that was a problem.

As they moved toward the house, the activity in the yard continued around them. Reuben noticed several men glance their way, their expressions ranging from curiosity to something less welcoming. One face in particular caught his attention—Dan Beachy, standing near the damaged outbuilding, watching their progress with undisguised suspicion.

Reuben's stomach tightened. Of all the people to encounter

here, Dan Beachy was perhaps the worst possible. John Beachy was something of a pest at the wedding, but mostly just all talk. But his father, Dan, held a deeper grudge than his son's hurt feelings over Nan's rejection. The man had connections to Lancaster, to people who remembered what had happened there. People who blamed Reuben.

Dan leaned toward another worker, speaking quietly. The man's eyebrows rose, and he glanced toward Reuben with new interest. The whispering had begun already.

Walking beside Reuben, Tommy noticed his sudden tension. "Reuben? Are you okay?"

Reuben forced his expression to neutralize. "Fine," he assured the boy, placing a hand on his shoulder. "Just tired from the journey. And there's still much to do."

As they neared the porch, Reuben overheard fragments of conversation from a group working nearby.

"…same one from Lancaster, I heard."

"…modernized equipment failed…"

"…whole farm lost…"

He stiffened, the familiar shame burning through him. Five years had passed, yet the whispers followed still. They always would, he supposed.

Nan had reached the steps but paused, looking back as if sensing his distress. Her brow furrowed with concern, but he couldn't meet her eyes. Instead, he focused on maintaining a calm exterior as they entered the farmhouse.

Inside, the large kitchen bustled with activity. Several women worked alongside Rose and *Tante* Lena, preparing what appeared to be an evening meal for the many volunteers. The familiar domestic scene, with its warmth and purposeful movement, only heightened Reuben's feeling of displacement.

"Sit, sit," *Grossmammi* Esther insisted, directing them to the table where a pitcher of water and cups awaited. "Tell us about your journey."

As Nan began recounting their trip—the obstacles they'd overcome, the devastation they'd witnessed—Reuben found himself watching her. Her face was animated with the telling, her hands gesturing to illustrate particularly challenging moments. Several times she mentioned his role—always giving him a degree of credit he didn't feel he deserved.

Each mention of his name drew more attention his way, increasing his discomfort.

"Reuben knew exactly what to do at every turn," Nan was saying, her blue eyes bright with an admiration he didn't deserve. "Without him, I'd never have gotten help for *Datt* or reached you so quickly."

Grossmammi Esther nodded, her wise gaze resting on him with uncomfortable perception.

Before Reuben could respond, Vernon entered the kitchen with an update on the ongoing work. "I have good news. My son-in-law has already made arrangements to evacuate the Elliots. The Virginia National Guard is on the way," he reported. "I knew you'd want to know."

"What of other families in Promise?" Nan asked. "Are they all safe?"

"So far, all accounted for," Vernon confirmed. "Some properties suffered worse damage than others. Eli Weaver is making rounds as best as he can to check on everyone. With the roads destroyed in so many places, he's recruited help from your congregation who can travel on horseback. I believe Martin Beiler knows many of the farmers because of his beehives. The Miller farm lost two outbuildings completely, and the Yoder place is dealing with significant flooding of their lower fields. But no lives lost, *dank sei Gott*."

"And *Datt*?" Nan's concern for her father remained evident despite the good news they'd received by radio. "Any new word?"

"Stable and receiving good care," Vernon assured her. "The hospital reports that the surgery on his leg went well."

As the conversation continued around him, Reuben found his gaze drawn to the window. Outside, Dan Beachy had positioned himself where he could observe the kitchen, his expression unreadable at this distance but his attention unmistakably focused on the house.

The walls seemed to close in slightly. Reuben's hands, resting on his knees beneath the table, curled into fists, then deliberately relaxed as he forced himself to appear calm.

When a lull in conversation finally came, he rose from the table. "I should check on Solomon and Buttercup." He grasped at the excuse.

"Oh, Lukas has already seen to them," Rose spoke up, her soft voice unusually quick. A faint blush colored her cheeks as she added, "He's very good with horses."

"Even so," Reuben insisted, edging toward the door. "I should make sure Solomon is settled. He can be particular with strangers."

Nan started to rise as if to accompany him, but he shook his head slightly. "Rest," he urged. "You've had a long day."

Something like hurt flickered across her face before she masked it, settling back into her chair.

The distance between them yawned wider, slowly undoing all that had connected them through the distress of the past days. Reuben felt it keenly yet couldn't bridge it. Not here, not with so many eyes watching and memories of Lancaster hovering like ghosts.

He slipped outside, relief flooding him as the open air replaced the kitchen's closeness.

He'd almost reached the barn when a voice called out behind him.

Dan Beachy approached, his expression carefully neutral but his posture hostile. "I see you've inserted yourself right into everyone's business here," he said, his tone just shy of openly confrontational.

"I'm helping where needed," Reuben replied evenly. "As are you."

"The difference," Dan countered, "is that no one questions whether my presence might bring more harm than good."

Reuben resisted the urge to clench his fists again. "If you have something to say, Dan, say it plainly."

"Very well." The older man stepped closer, lowering his voice. "My cousin Isaiah lost everything when your modern equipment failed in Lancaster. His entire herd, generations of careful breeding, gone because you thought you knew better than tradition." His eyes hardened. "Now here you are again, in the middle of another disaster. Seems to follow you, doesn't it?"

Before Reuben could respond, another voice interrupted.

"Is there a problem here?" Vernon Mast approached from the direction of the barn, his expression making it clear he'd observed the confrontation.

Dan stepped back, shaking his head. "No problem, Bishop. Just exchanging information about storm damage." With a final meaningful look at Reuben, he returned to his work group.

Vernon watched him go, then turned to Reuben. "Don't let him trouble you. He seems quick to judge and slow to forgive."

"He's not entirely wrong," Reuben said quietly. "About Lancaster."

"Perhaps not," Vernon acknowledged. "But five years is a long time to carry such judgment against a man." He studied Reuben thoughtfully. "Your warning saved lives this time, Reuben. That counts for something in the greater balance."

Before Reuben could reply, Vernon continued, "Jake and Aubrey should arrive tomorrow, if the roads continue to clear. Until then, there's a place for you in the bunkhouse we've set up in the barn loft, but I believe the boys have their hearts set on you staying with them in Jake and Aubrey's cabin. That's where Lukas has been staying, I understand."

"I reckon that settles it, then. Tommy and Daniel win out." Reuben couldn't help but smile at the mention of the two boys, but itched for a moment alone. "I'll see to my mule now, if you'll excuse me."

In the barn, Reuben found Solomon contentedly munching hay in a clean stall, indeed well tended as Rose had said. The familiar task of checking the animal over gave his hands purpose while his mind churned with conflicting emotions.

The past days with Nan, he'd allowed himself to imagine a different future, one where his past mistakes didn't define him completely.

But if the reality that reasserted itself the moment they'd arrived at the farm wasn't enough, Dan Beachy's presence was another much needed reminder of why Reuben maintained his distance from others. His failure in Lancaster hadn't harmed only himself—it had affected families like Isaiah Beachy's, destroyed livelihoods built over generations.

And now Nan looked at him with eyes that saw possibility, not ruin. It wasn't fair to her. She deserved someone untainted by such a past, someone who could move unjudged among the people she so clearly loved.

Solomon nudged his arm, breaking his grim reverie. The mule's liquid brown eyes held no judgment, only the simple expectation of care.

"At least you're easy to please," Reuben murmured, stroking the animal's strong neck.

From outside came the sound of children's laughter—Tommy and Daniel playing with some of the other youngsters despite the day's challenges. Above, the late afternoon sun slanted through the barn windows, painting golden rectangles across the straw-covered floor.

Life continued, regardless of his private turmoil. The community would rebuild, as it always did after hardship. Tomorrow would bring more work, more decisions. And eventually, Reuben knew, a choice he couldn't postpone indefinitely—no matter how much he dreaded it.

For now, though, he would focus on the simple task before him. The rest would have to wait.

Through the window, Nan could see Reuben speaking with Vernon Mast near the damaged outbuilding. Even from this distance, she could read the tension in his posture—the stiff set of his shoulders, the careful distance he maintained. Nothing like the man who had ridden beside her through the devastated countryside, who had shared insights about his solitude and his past, who had boosted her onto Buttercup with such gentle strength.

Nan kneaded the bread dough with perhaps more force than necessary, pushing her frustration into the resilient mass beneath her palms. The kitchen hummed with activity as women cleaned the dishes from the evening meal for the many volunteers.

Cassie had arrived to help just before the meal and worked beside her, preparing the loaves to rise overnight to feed the crowd the following day.

"You're going to flatten that poor dough entirely," Cassie observed. "I think it's surrendered."

Nan looked down, realizing she'd been working the same portion of dough for far too long. "Sorry," she murmured, shaping it quickly into a ball and covering it with a cloth to rise overnight.

Her best friend's shrewd eyes missed nothing. "He's a complicated man, that one."

"Who?" Nan asked, feigning ignorance though she knew perfectly well whom she meant.

Cassie's mouth quirked with amusement. "The one you've

been watching through the window for the past ten minutes." She took over preparing the next loaf. "There's always been a spark between you two. Sometimes not so much for the best, but you can't say you've ever been indifferent about each other."

"*Nay*, not on my part," Nan admitted, "but I always thought Reuben actually disliked me until... Well, through the storm he was..." She hesitated, searching for the right word. "Different. More open, somehow. And..."

"And now he's drawn back like a turtle into its shell," Cassie observed. "And you don't like that."

"That about sums it up." Nan never could hide anything from Cassie. She was the one friend who had always accepted Nan, faults and all. And Nan loved her dearly for it.

"Tell me about the storm," Nan said, changing the subject. "What was it like in town?"

Cassie accepted the shift with grace. "At first, we were so busy that I didn't have time to be frightened. We've weathered many storms before. But when the winds grew stronger than I'd ever heard..." She paused, her expression sobering. "Martin, well, you know how matter-of-fact he always is, so he had noticed his bees preparing for a storm days earlier. So he didn't panic. He had a plan ready to go. If the bees were sealing up their hives, he figured he ought to be doing the same. By the time I got to the cottage, he'd boarded up the windows and sandbagged the doors to keep out water. He said the only thing left to do was pray for wisdom and mercy."

Nan squeezed her friend's hand. "And I know that you were a rock for him, too. I worried so about you. About everyone. I've never felt so helpless."

"It is difficult to explain, *ya*. Feeling so helpless, yet sensing *Gott*'s presence surrounding you, even in those dangerous hours..." Cassie's voice trailed off, as she swiped at a tear. "Others have suffered so much more. I can be here to help, but they... like your *datt*," she stuttered before drawing a deep breath, then looking Nan directly in the eye. "He's going to be okay. I just know he is. And we will all get through this."

Cassie's sweet confidence was like a balm Nan hadn't known she needed.

"*Ya*, we will." Nan hugged Cassie from the side. "Together."

Just as Nan dried a tear of her own and reached for another piece of dough to knead, *Tante* Lena approached. "The *kinner* would like to spend the night at their own cabin tonight with Lukas and Reuben," she announced, tapping Nan on the shoulder. "Perhaps you could check on things. Make sure they have what they need in the cabin. Take Reuben's supper to him while you're at it. Hmm?"

What could they need that her sister Aubrey wouldn't have already made sure was in their new home? And Nan was about to ask, but Cassie bumped her shoulder and whispered, "Go on. Take the hint."

Tante Lena was a shrewd one when it came to matchmaking. And this time, even her best friend was chiming in, yet somehow, she didn't mind.

Nan wiped her hands quickly on her apron and slipped outside. The evening air had cooled considerably, stars emerging in the early twilight. Her gaze swept the yard, finally spotting Reuben's powerful tall figure working alone in the smaller barn where Jake stored equipment for the sunflower farm.

She approached quietly, pausing at the open doorway. Reuben was methodically cleaning and organizing tools, his back to the entrance.

"You missed supper," she said simply.

His shoulders tensed slightly, but he didn't turn around. "I wasn't hungry."

"*Grossmammi* set aside a plate for you."

"*Denki*. Perhaps later." He hadn't looked up to see the plate in her hand.

Nan stepped into the barn, moving where he would have to

acknowledge her presence. "You've been avoiding me since we arrived."

Now he did look at her, his expression guarded. "I've been helping where needed."

"Alone," she pointed out. "When there are dozens of people working together just yards away."

Reuben set down the tool he'd been cleaning. "I work better that way."

"That's not what I've seen the past couple of days." Her frustration broke through. "You were…different. You talked to me, really talked. We solved problems together. What changed the moment we arrived?"

He turned away again, arranging tools with unnecessary precision. "Nothing changed. We did what was necessary to reach the farm safely. Now we're here, and other arrangements make more sense."

"Other arrangements?" She stepped closer. "You mean walls. Barriers. Distance."

"Call it what you like." His voice remained steady, but she saw the tension in his hands. "It doesn't change reality."

"Which reality? The one where you helped save lives by warning of the storm? The one where you risked yourself to bring my *datt* to safety? Or the one you've imagined where you deserve to be alone because of something that happened years ago?"

Reuben's movements stilled. "You don't know what happened in Lancaster."

"Then tell me," she challenged. "Help me understand why Dan Beachy looks at you with such judgment. Why you pull away whenever anyone tries to come close."

For a moment, she thought he might actually answer. Something in his appearance mellowed, an opening appearing in the careful mask. But then his gaze moved past her to the doorway, and his expression shuttered again.

"Some mistakes can't be undone, Nan," he said finally, his voice low and controlled. "Some consequences must be carried. It's simplest if I carry mine alone."

The defeat in his tone sparked a surprising anger in her. "Simplest or just safer? You hide in your library with your books and your weather journals, recording patterns and making predictions. But what good is all that knowledge if you never use it to help others?"

His eyes snapped back to hers, a flare of emotion breaking through. "I did use it. I warned your *datt* and the other bishops about the storm."

"Yes, you did," she acknowledged, though not sorry the barb gained his full attention. "And how many lives were saved because of that warning? How many people reached safety because you shared what you knew instead of keeping yourself locked away? But why stop now? Why shut yourself off again? From us…from *me*?"

He knew what she was asking. She knew he did by the flicker in his eyes and the slight wince at the reference to herself.

But before he could respond, the patter of small feet approached the barn, and Tommy's voice called out, "*Tante* Nan? Reuben?"

The moment shattered. Reuben's expression closed again as both boys appeared in the doorway.

"Are you coming to stay with us, Reuben?" Tommy spoke for both boys, while Daniel wrapped his arms around Reuben's leg. "And *Tante* Lena said Nan would tell us a story."

"We're coming," Nan assured them, though her eyes remained on Reuben.

"You go on ahead," he said to the boys, presumably hoping Nan would go, too. "I have a few things to finish here."

Tommy frowned. "But you're supposed to say prayers with us."

Reuben hesitated, clearly torn between his desire for solitude and the boy's expectation. Daniel moved to stand beside his brother, both watching with hopeful expressions.

"*Kumm* now, puh-weez." Daniel's sweetness stirred her heart.

And seemed to reach Reuben in a way Nan's arguments couldn't. He set down the tool he'd been holding and nodded slowly.

"*Oll recht*, I'll be right there."

The boys grinned, then scampered jubilantly toward their cabin, and Nan reluctantly turned to follow. Reuben was by her side in one long stride, blocking her exit.

"It's not that simple," he said softly, continuing their interrupted conversation. "What happened in Lancaster—"

"I know it's not simple," she interrupted gently. "But you don't have to face it alone."

He didn't respond, but neither did he pull away when her hand brushed his arm in the dim light of the barn. For one heartbeat, then two, they stood together in a fragile moment of connection.

Then he stepped aside, gesturing for her to precede him out of the barn. "They're waiting," he said simply.

As they walked toward the cabin, where lamplight spilled from the windows, Nan studied Reuben's profile. The walls had risen again, but perhaps not quite as high as before. A single step taken, with many more needed.

At the porch steps, he paused to let her go first. For several heartbeats after he opened the door for her, he remained motionless, his face unreadable in the soft lamplight. Then, drawing a deep breath, he crossed the threshold.

One step, perhaps, but significant, as he joined the *kinner* for the night.

And Nan, watching him find his place beside the waiting children, allowed herself to hope that it might be only the first of many such steps toward sharing more in their lives.

And maybe even in hers.

Chapter Thirteen

Reuben woke before dawn. A full night's sleep in a real bed brought a momentary comfort that quickly faded as he recalled the events of the past few days—the storm, the bishop's rescue, and now the daunting task of helping an entire community rebuild.

Sleep had come fitfully at first because of the gnawing certainty that his past in Lancaster would soon collide with his present in Promise. Every time he closed his eyes, he saw Dan Beachy's knowing looks, heard the barely disguised insinuations about his "previous failures." It was only a matter of time before everyone knew.

Before Nan knew.

Reuben rose quietly, careful not to disturb the sleeping *kinner* who were snuggled together on the small bed on the other side of the room, then made his way from the loft to the kitchen below. The gray predawn light filtered through the window.

Outside, the first hints of sunrise painted the sky in pale pinks and golds. The air felt clean after the storm—a deceptive freshness that belied the destruction visible in every direction. Fallen trees, waterlogged fields and debris scattered across what had once been neatly tended farmland. Yet somehow, the Burkholder farmhouse and this cabin had remained standing, becoming a natural gathering point for rescue and recovery operations.

The sound of voices drew his attention to the outdoor summer kitchen, where several Amish women were already preparing breakfast for the growing number of volunteers. Reuben hesitated, scanning the faces. Nan wasn't among them.

He turned away, needing a few more moments alone before facing everyone. Bending over the sink, he splashed cold water on his face, clearing the last cobwebs of sleep from his mind.

"Good morning." Vernon Mast's deep voice startled him. "Just making my rounds to rally everyone for breakfast."

Reuben straightened, water dripping from his beard, as he turned to see the man holding the door open and peeking his head inside.

"Goot mariye," Reuben replied, reaching for the small towel hanging on a nearby hook.

"I hope you got some rest," Vernon said. "We have much work ahead today."

Reuben nodded. "What needs to be done first?"

Vernon's face creased with a smile. "Always straight to business with you. That's why I've been thinking..." He paused, seeming to reconsider his words. "But that's for later. This morning, we need to assess the eastern fields of the Burkholder property. I understand from Rose that their main sunflower crop was planted there."

"Sure, I can check the fields," Reuben offered. "They're likely to have significant flooding, given the way the creek curves around that section."

"Actually," Vernon replied, "I'd like you to check the small lake and dam on the Burkholder property. With all this rainfall, I'm concerned about its stability. If that dam were to fail, it could create more flooding." Reuben tensed, memories of Lancaster filling his mind.

"So you'd prefer me to check the dam? I'm not sure how qualified I am."

"You're the most knowledgeable person we have, until experts from the state can arrive," Vernon insisted. "And I'd like you to take Nan with you—she knows the family's land better than any of the volunteers."

A mixture of anticipation and dread settled in Reuben's stomach. Time alone with Nan would once have been unthinkable—now it was both what he most wanted and most feared.

"I'll find her," Reuben said, though his voice lacked conviction. "Just as soon as Rose comes to get the *kinner*."

Vernon clapped him on the shoulder. "After breakfast. Everyone needs strength for the day ahead."

Rose showed up soon after to care for Tommy and Daniel, so Lukas and Reuben could get to work. The meal was served outdoors on makeshift tables constructed from boards laid across sawhorses. The community of volunteers and the Burkholders gathered, heads bowed in silent prayer before the simple breakfast of oatmeal, bread and preserved fruit was passed around.

Reuben found himself seated between Vernon and one of the younger men from the neighboring district. Across from him, Dan Beachy spoke animatedly with several others.

Dan wasn't speaking directly to him, wasn't even looking his way, but the snippets he could overhear were clear enough. The past wasn't forgotten, and Dan wasn't going to let others forget either.

"Good news," Vernon announced, his voice cutting through the murmur of conversations. "We've received word that Jake and Aubrey will indeed get here today."

A ripple of pleasure moved through the group. Jake's return would mean another strong back for the work, but more than that, it represented a small step toward normalcy—the newly married couple returning home to help.

"Teams for today." Vernon's loud voice commanded attention, as he pulled a small notebook from his pocket. "Miller and Yoder families will work on clearing the main road. Byler and Lapp men are packing supplies to be delivered to neighboring farms. Reuben and Nan will assess the dam while Rose and Lukas check the sunflower fields. The rest of us will continue to assess the local needs more and prioritize the most serious ones, like delivering medications and water."

As assignments continued, Reuben searched the gathering for Nan. He found her sitting with Rose and her grandmother, her golden hair neatly pinned beneath her white *kapp*. She looked tired but somehow energized, leaning forward as she listened to Vernon's instructions. When her name was paired with his, her gaze immediately found him across the tables, and she gave a small nod of acknowledgment.

"Don't suppose the *Englisch* will have electricity back anytime soon." Dan Beachy's voice carried as people began to disperse after breakfast. "Reminds me of that summer storm that knocked out power to half of Lancaster County. Some weren't prepared for that, either."

Reuben froze, the comment striking its intended target with precision. His fingers tightened around his coffee cup.

Vernon responded matter-of-factly. "The power company estimates weeks, possibly longer for the remote areas. But we're accustomed to managing without, unlike our neighbors."

"Ya," Dan agreed, his eyes sliding toward Reuben. "Though some of us relied more on modern conveniences than others. Great until they fail, ain't so?"

Reuben fought the impulse to respond. A confrontation would only draw more attention. He stood, gathering his plate and utensils, and made his way toward the washing station.

"I'll meet you by the cabin path that leads down to the lake in about ten minutes." Nan's voice came from just behind him, startling him from his thoughts.

He turned to find her watching him, her expression a mixture of concern and determination. Had she heard Dan's comments? Could she read the tension in his shoulders, the careful control he was maintaining?

"*Ya*, fine," he managed.

"I'll bring a notepad to map the damage," she continued, graciously willing to let the topic of his discomfort slide.

Reuben nodded, grateful. "*Goot* thinking."

"And Reuben?" She stepped closer, lowering her voice. "Jake and Aubrey are coming. That's *goot* news, *ya*?"

"Ya," he agreed, tension easing slightly at the thought of his cousin's arrival. "That is *goot* news."

A smile touched her lips, and for a moment, the weight on his shoulders lightened. Whatever revelations the day might bring, at least in this moment, Nan was looking at him with something like trust in her eyes.

"Ten minutes," she repeated, already turning away toward the house.

Reuben watched her go, knowing that soon enough, she would learn the truth about his past. The question that haunted him was whether she would look at him the same way afterward.

Fifteen minutes later, they set out toward the lake at the far edge of the Burkholder property, each carrying supplies for their assessment. The path that normally provided easy access was now littered with fallen branches and debris. In places, the saturated ground had given way entirely, forcing them to find alternative routes.

As they walked, Reuben found himself cataloging the damage with the farmer's eye he'd inherited from generations before him. Everything he saw spoke to the tremendous force of the flood waters.

"The lake has been here since before my *dawdi*'s time," Nan explained as they made their way carefully along a ridge. "During the Great Depression it was dug out to provide irrigation during dry summers, and the small dam was built to control water flow downstream."

Reuben nodded, his throat tight. Dams. Water control. The very things that had led to catastrophe in Lancaster.

"Sensible planning," he managed to say.

They stopped at an outcropping with a full view of the lake below them. What had once been a modest body of water had transformed into a swollen, debris-filled pool that strained against its boundaries. The dam at the far end was barely visible beneath the churning water that poured over its top.

"It's overtopped," Reuben said, immediately alert to the danger. "Vernon will need to let state officials know right away." He only hoped that with all the other emergency situations, someone would be available to help soon.

Nan's eyes widened as she grasped his concern.

He eased closer to the edge of the lake, studying the way the water moved against the earthen embankment. His experienced eye could see signs of seepage—wet spots appearing on the downstream face of the dam where water was finding its way through.

"We need to check the spillway," he said, already moving toward the structure. "If it's blocked by debris, the pressure on the dam itself will increase."

Nan followed, notebook clutched in her hand. "What should I record?"

"Water levels. Points of seepage. Any visible cracks or bulges in the earthen portions." This was something he could potentially prevent from becoming a disaster by giving accurate information to the authorities. "I'll tell you what to write as we go."

As they carefully made their way around the lake's perimeter, Reuben pointed out concerning signs—places where water had begun to erode the dam's structure or sections where overflow had carved away supporting soil.

"Jake and Aubrey will bring this place back again. And your

lavender fields, Reuben," Nan said as they worked. "We can restore them, too."

We?

Reuben didn't respond immediately, his heart yearning to believe she was right. Wishing her reference to them both was more than a fairy tale of an idea. If only he could believe so as readily as Nan.

He fixed his gaze on the lake rather than meet the purity of hope in her eyes and tamped down the memory of the greenhouse full of lavender slips that Nan had rescued from his burned-out fields. The same ones that now resembled a swamp.

He couldn't see the future she saw. But Jake would arrive soon. That was a relief. Both Vernon and his cousin had confidence in him. It didn't make much difference, though, not when Dan Beachy was systematically laying the groundwork for revealing Reuben's greatest shame.

Time was running out on the fragile bond he'd formed with Nan during the crisis. Soon enough, she would learn what happened in Lancaster. And then she would understand why he had kept his distance all these years.

Why he didn't deserve second chances.

Nan stepped carefully around a fallen branch, notebook clutched in one hand, her gaze sweeping across the troubled waters. "What can be done?"

"Sandbags might help temporarily," he replied, his mind seemingly already calculating quantities and placement. "And clearing the spillway of debris. But proper repairs will require equipment we don't have right now."

He had grown quiet, contemplative as he assessed the dam from various angles.

And she let him remain that way. At least for a bit. And suddenly she realized she was changing, too. It wasn't in her nature to leave things unspoken. *Nay*, she wanted everything out in the open. Exposed to the light.

But for Reuben she was learning that he needed time. He needed a measure of privacy. And somehow she was able to give it to him.

They moved along the edge of the dam, carefully documenting the damage. Nan drew a rough map as they went, marking the worst areas and those with potential for immediate intervention.

"The main flow overtopped here," he explained, indicating a section where debris had piled high against the concrete spillway. "But the water finding its way through the earthen portions is more concerning. See how the soil's been carved away in channels? That's water finding weaknesses in the structure."

Nan nodded, unable to hide her admiration for his expertise. "How did you ever learn so much?"

Reuben stiffened slightly, his momentary openness receding. "Experience teaches hard lessons," he said, his voice dropping. "I've seen what water can do when underestimated."

The change was subtle but unmistakable—like a door slowly closing.

"Reuben." She closed her notebook, making a decision she'd been contemplating since overhearing those breakfast table insinuations. "Will you tell me what happened? In Lancaster? I want to understand."

She always wanted to know things. But this time, she truly only wanted to understand. For his sake. Not her own.

His head snapped up, amber eyes widening slightly before his expression closed completely. "*Nay*, Nan. It doesn't matter now."

"It does matter," she insisted, taking a step closer. "Whatever happened there is still with you. I can see it—especially when Dan Beachy speaks."

"Dan Beachy enjoys other people's misfortunes," Reuben muttered.

"That may be so. But there's more to it than that." She gentled her voice. "You helped me when I needed it most. Let me help you now."

He continued walking, his broad shoulders set in a rigid line as he moved. When he finally spoke, his voice was so low she had to strain to hear it.

"Why do you want to know, Nan? What good would it do?"

"Because whatever it is, it's like a wall between you and everyone else. Even when you're standing right beside me, there's always a distance." She paused, gathering courage for what she truly wanted to say. "Especially since we've returned to the farm."

Reuben stopped abruptly, his back still toward her. For a long moment, the only sound was the distant call of birds.

"It was my fault," he said finally, his voice rough-edged. "All of it."

Nan remained silent, sensing that any interruption might cause him to stop. After several heartbeats, he turned to face her, his expression raw with a pain so long endured it had become part of him.

"My father died when I was nineteen," he began. "The dairy farm came to me. Fourth-generation Bender to run it." His gaze drifted beyond her, as if seeing those distant fields instead of the devastation surrounding them. "I had ideas. Modern ideas. Ways to make the farm more efficient, more productive."

He drew a deep breath, his hands clenching and unclenching at his sides.

"Some of the elders were concerned, but I was young and certain. My grandfather had bought mechanical milking machines when others still milked by hand. My father had added refrigeration when others used ice houses. Why shouldn't I move us forward, as well?"

Nan nodded. Many Amish communities had adopted some

technologies for farming while maintaining simpler lifestyles otherwise.

"I installed an automated flooring system, a new invention to move the cattle through the process faster, more efficiently," Reuben continued. "Electric powered, with backup generators for when storms knocked out utility power. It was expensive, but neighbors invested—Isaiah Beachy's family among them. They believed in my vision for the future."

The connection to Dan Beachy suddenly became clear. Nan's stomach tightened with apprehension.

"There was a storm," she guessed softly.

Reuben nodded, a muscle working in his jaw. "Worse than predicted. It knocked out power across three counties. The backup generators should have engaged automatically, but..." His voice faltered. "A relay switch failed. We were stuck with equipment we couldn't repair ourselves because it was too sophisticated. And then flooding caused irreparable damage. The entire system was destroyed. The flooring collapsed while fully loaded."

"The cows," Nan whispered, horrified understanding dawning.

"We lost them. The herd my grandfather and father had spent decades developing," Reuben confirmed, voice hollow with remembered anguish. "So much suffering that could have been avoided if I'd only..."

He trailed off, turning away again with shoulders hunched as if physically carrying the weight of his guilt.

"The financial losses were catastrophic," he continued after a moment. "Not just for my family, but for all who had invested. The Beachys lost their savings. The Stoltzfus family had to sell land that had been theirs for generations."

Nan moved closer, her heart aching for the young man he'd been, suddenly facing such devastating consequences.

"You couldn't have known the equipment would fail," she offered gently. "You couldn't stop the storm."

"I should have listened to the elders who warned against relying too heavily on technology we couldn't control ourselves. My pride cost others everything, Nan."

The rawness in his voice—clearly still haunted by the destruction he witnessed—struck her deeply. He was once again that young man who had carried the responsibility for his own family and others in his community and believed he had failed them all.

"So you left," she said softly.

Reuben nodded. "There was nothing left for me there. The farm was sold to cover debts. My mother went to live with her sister in Ohio." His expression grew distant once more. "I wandered for a time. My woodworking hobby helped to make ends meet. Then I heard about land for sale in Promise. Thought perhaps I could start again, far from those I'd hurt. With lavender instead of dairy—simpler, less risk to others."

"And then the fire," Nan added, understanding deepening.

"*Ya*. Another failure." His bitter laugh held no humor. "Perhaps Dan Beachy is right to remind everyone of my past. I seem destined to bring disaster wherever I go."

Impulsively, Nan reached out, her hand finding his arm. "That's not true, Reuben. The fire wasn't your fault. And what happened in Lancaster was a terrible accident, not deliberate harm."

"Intent matters little to those who suffered the consequences," he replied, though he didn't pull away from her touch.

"So you've been punishing yourself all these years," she said, the realization bringing a wave of compassion. "Keeping apart, refusing to let anyone close. Living as if you don't deserve friendship or—" She stopped herself before finishing that thought.

Reuben's gaze met hers, a flicker of dying hope passing

through his amber eyes. "Everyone is better off without my interference."

"*Nay*, that's not true," Nan insisted. "Look at what happened during the storm. Your knowledge saved lives, Reuben. My father might have died if not for you."

He shook his head, though with less certainty than before.

For a moment, Nan thought she might have reached him—might have finally breached the wall he'd built around himself.

"This dam needs attention, Nan." His abrupt change made her head spin. "Soon. The spillway is partially blocked, and there's significant erosion on the back side. If we get another heavy rain before it's repaired…"

He didn't finish the sentence. He didn't need to. They both understood what failure would mean. And he was right. They had no time to spare.

As they started back toward the farmhouse, Nan couldn't help feeling they'd left something unfinished behind them.

"Reuben," she said, stopping him with a hand on his sleeve. "What happened in Lancaster doesn't change how I see you. If anything, I understand you better now."

He studied her face, seeming to search for something in her expression. Whatever he found—or didn't find—caused a shadow to cross his features.

"You're kind to say so," he replied, his voice carefully neutral. "But others won't share your generous view."

"You can't know that," she protested.

"I know Dan Beachy," he countered grimly. "And once the full story emerges, the rest will follow."

With a final glance at her, Reuben set off toward the farmhouse, his long strides eating up the distance. Nan followed, troubled by the sense that he'd made a choice in those moments—one she wasn't going to like.

As they crested the small rise that led back to the farm buildings, she saw a small crowd gathered in the yard. Jake and Aubrey stood at its center, travel-worn but smiling as they greeted everyone. Tommy and Daniel hovered close to their aunt and uncle, clearly relieved by their return.

What should have been a joyful reunion, however, seemed overshadowed by tension—and not only because of the urgency of their discoveries at the lake.

Even from a distance, Nan could see Dan Beachy standing to one side, as he watched the proceedings with narrowed eyes. Then she caught Dan's expression change as he noticed Reuben approaching, from calculating to the satisfaction of a man about to settle an old score. And a cold chill ran down her spine.

Reuben shouldn't have unburdened himself to Nan. For years, he'd carried the story of Lancaster within him, speaking of it to no one in Promise except Jake. Now Nan knew, and while her immediate reaction had been kinder than he deserved, he couldn't shake the certainty that her opinion would change once she had time to fully consider the implications of his failure.

Still, there had been that moment—that brief, shining moment when she'd looked at him with compassion rather than judgment, when she'd touched his arm and insisted the past didn't define him. It was more than he had allowed himself to hope for. And more than he could allow himself to enjoy, not while knowing what was bound to come next.

Jake stood in the center of the yard, one arm around Aubrey, the other gesturing as he described their journey. His cousin looked weary but relieved to be back, his usual good humor evident even at a distance. Aubrey leaned into him, her face bright despite obvious exhaustion.

At their feet, Tommy and Daniel hovered like satellites around a planet, clearly unwilling to stray too far from the aunt and uncle who had become their world.

Jake looked up, a broad smile spreading across his face as he spotted his cousin. “Reuben! So great to see you!”

He strode forward, Aubrey at his side, to embrace Reuben in a bear hug that nearly lifted him off his feet. “These two rascals have been telling everyone how you rescued the bishop and had him saved by a helicopter at your cabin.”

“They exaggerate,” Reuben replied, discomfort rising at being the center of attention.

“Perhaps a little,” Aubrey agreed with a warm smile, reaching out to clasp his hands in hers. “But *Datt* says otherwise. We were able to speak with him by phone at a stop on our way. And the doctor reports he’s recovering well, thanks to your quick action.”

Reuben inclined his head, accepting her gratitude without comment. Over her shoulder, he noticed Dan Beachy watching their exchange, his expression unreadable. A familiar wariness came over him.

“How was your journey?” he asked Jake, deliberately turning his back on Dan.

“Long,” Jake admitted. “But some helpful guardsmen got us through areas where roads are gone completely. The damage gets worse as you go south.” His expression sobered. “The North Carolina mountains and parts of southeastern Tennessee took the brunt of it. Entire communities cut off.”

“Ya,” Vernon agreed, joining their circle. “That’s what I’ve been hearing on the emergency radio. They need experienced help down there—volunteers who understand mountain terrain and can work without modern equipment.”

Nan appeared beside Aubrey, and the two sisters embraced warmly. Reuben couldn’t help but notice how Nan’s gaze kept flickering toward him, a worried crease between her brows. Had she already begun to reconsider her earlier compassion? Or was she concerned about what Dan might say?

“Vernon’s been telling us about the Mennonite Aid Society's plans," Jake continued, unaware of the tension building around them. "They're forming teams to head south as soon as the roads are passable."

The moment seemed a good opportunity to warn Vernon and Jake both about the condition of the dam and the need for urgent help.

"I'll send a report to my son-in-law, right away." Vernon's brow wrinkled with concern. "He works full-time in emergency management and will know how to get this to the right authorities." He turned to Jake. "Rest assured, he won't quit until someone is on their way to deal with this."

Dan Beachy stepped forward, inserting himself into the conversation. "Some have more experience with water damage than others, ain't so?"

The deliberate nod in Reuben's direction wasn't lost on anyone. A ripple of awkward silence spread through the gathered group.

"That's true," Vernon replied evenly. "Which is why I've been hoping to convince Reuben to join one of our relief teams heading to North Carolina."

Reuben's head snapped up in surprise. "Me?"

"Ya," Vernon confirmed, seemingly oblivious to Dan's insinuation. "It would be for several months—the hardest hit areas will need skilled help through the fall at least. Jake will be leading our team here. I'd like you on another in the Carolinas."

The offer caught Reuben by surprise. He had expected to help with the immediate recovery in Promise, of course, but the idea of joining an official relief effort, of working alongside others in a strange community for months—it was so far outside what he had allowed himself to consider that he struggled to formulate a response.

"Reuben's skills would certainly be valuable," Dan interjected before he could speak. "As long as there's no electricity involved."

The pointed comment landed like a stone in still water, sending ripples of confusion through those gathered. Jake's expression darkened with recognition of what was coming, while most others merely looked puzzled.

Dan smiled thinly. "Perhaps your neighbor should explain his expertise with electrical failures."

"Dan," Jake warned, stepping forward. "This isn't the time or place."

"When would be better?" Dan countered. "Before or after he's sent to help people who don't know his history? People who might trust him with decisions that affect their livelihoods?"

The circle of onlookers had grown, drawn by the rising tension in Dan's voice. Reuben stood frozen, watching as the moment he had dreaded for years unfolded before him. Nan moved closer to his side, her presence both comfort and further complication.

"Ask him about Lancaster," Dan pressed. "About his newfangled system that failed during a storm and cost dozens of families their savings. Ask him about my cousin Isaiah's family, who lost everything because they trusted Reuben Bender's *modern ideas*."

The accusations hung in the air, stark and damning. Reuben felt rather than saw the shift in those around him—the subtle withdrawing, the exchange of glances, the reassessment of everything they thought they knew.

"Let the man speak for himself or be quiet," Vernon reprimanded Dan then turned to Reuben.

For a moment, Reuben considered denial. But the lie would only postpone the inevitable, and he had spent too many years living with the weight of his actions to add dishonesty to his burden now.

"There's nothing to say." Reuben accepted defeat, his voice steady despite the turmoil within. "It's true."

A murmur rippled through the gathering. Jake moved to

stand beside him, a silent declaration of support, while Aubrey's expression registered shocked recognition.

"It was years ago," Jake began, but Dan cut him off.

"Time doesn't change what happened," he snapped. "And they should know that I've already sent word to my relatives in Lancaster that Reuben is involved in recovery efforts here. Isaiah and the others have a right to know he's positioning himself as some kind of expert on disaster recovery."

"That's not what's happening," Vernon objected. "We're simply trying to organize the most effective help—"

"Six families lost their investments," Dan continued, speaking over Vernon as if he hadn't heard. "And Reuben Bender disappeared rather than face the consequences."

Each word struck Reuben like a physical blow. In Dan's telling, he was not just responsible but callous, fleeing accountability rather than fleeing the unbearable shame.

"That is not the whole truth," Jake protested, his voice rising with rare anger. "Reuben stayed until every debt was settled, until every family had received what could be salvaged from the sale of his property. He sold the farm that had been in his family for generations to make things right. He left with nothing but the clothes on his back."

"And his precious woodworking tools," Dan sneered.

The accusation struck home. Reuben had indeed kept his tools—the only means by which he could earn a living after the farm was gone. The tools had been his father's and grandfather's before him, the last connection to his family heritage.

Around him, the expressions of his neighbors told the story of his worst fears realized. Shock. Dismay. Even with Jake's defense, they were seeing him anew—not as the quiet, competent farmer they had known, but as a man whose reckless actions had caused widespread suffering.

His gaze found Nan almost against his will. Her blue eyes were wide with distress, her face pale. She took a step toward him, reaching out as if to offer comfort, but he stepped away to stop her.

Vernon cleared his throat, breaking the heavy silence. "Whatever happened in the past," he said firmly, "is in the past. And it doesn't change the fact that we need his help now. Reuben has demonstrated his knowledge, quick thinking and stamina during this current crisis. He's earned my respect, and I stand by my decision. Reuben will make an excellent team leader in the days ahead."

"And those who trust him will regret it, just as they did in Lancaster." With that parting shot, Dan walked away, the crowd parting before him like water around a stone.

In his wake, conversations erupted—hushed at first, then growing in volume as people discussed what they had heard.

"Reuben," Vernon began, his expression troubled. "I had no idea—"

"It's alright," Reuben interrupted, unable to bear sympathy on top of everything else. "Dan is correct about what happened. I made a terrible mistake that cost others dearly." He drew a deep breath. "I appreciate your offer, but I'm not the right person for your team."

"That's not true," Jake protested. "You're exactly the right person. Your experience—"

"Is precisely why I should stay away," Reuben finished for him. The weight that had briefly lifted over the past few days with Nan had returned tenfold, pressing down on him until breathing itself seemed an effort. "I've caused enough damage for one lifetime."

Tommy tugged at his sleeve, his young face creased with confusion. "Uncle Reuben? Why is that man mad at you?"

The innocent question nearly undid him. Reuben knelt to meet the boy at eye level, placing his hands on small shoulders. "Sometimes grown-ups make mistakes that hurt others," he explained gently. "And those mistakes have consequences that last a long time."

"But you helped us," Daniel insisted, joining his brother. "You saved *Dawdi* Naaman and fixed the path so the helicopter could come."

"That's different," Reuben tried to explain, though the words felt hollow even to him.

"Why?" Tommy demanded with a child's relentless logic. "If you made a mistake before, that doesn't mean you can't do good things now."

Out of the mouths of babes, Reuben thought, momentarily speechless. The very argument Nan had made, now echoed by a child who saw the world in simpler terms.

Before he could formulate a response, Vernon's hand came to rest on his shoulder. "The boys have a point," he said quietly. "None of us are defined solely by our worst moments."

"Some moments have longer shadows than others," Reuben replied, rising to his feet.

Around them, the crowd had begun to disperse, breaking into smaller groups that cast occasional glances their way. Reuben could almost feel the narrative spreading—the story of his failure traveling from person to person, coloring every interaction he would have from this point forward.

Jake, Aubrey and Nan remained steadfastly beside him, their presence a buffer against the worst of the scrutiny. But it wasn't enough. It could never be enough to counterbalance what he had set in motion all those years ago.

And now, with Dan's message already on its way to Lancaster, the circle would close completely. Any peace he had managed to construct in Promise would be shattered.

His gaze sought Nan's once more, finding her already watching—waiting—for him to seek her. Something passed between them—an acknowledgment, a question, a plea. He couldn't be sure which, only that it tugged at something within him that he had long believed dead.

"I need to check on the animals." He grasped at the same old excuse, turning away from the silent exchange. "Make sure they have fresh water."

Inside the barn the familiar scents of hay and livestock enveloped him, a momentary comfort that did nothing to ease the certainty growing within him.

There was only one path forward now.

He had to leave Promise.

Not for the relief mission Vernon had suggested, but permanently. His presence would only bring more pain, more division, more reminders of failure. Jake and the boys would be better off without the shadow he cast. Nan would be free to find someone worthy of her compassion, her insight, her growing affection.

The community would heal without him.

And he would carry his burden elsewhere, as he had done before.

As he had always known he would eventually have to do again.

Chapter Fourteen

The next day, seeking a moment's peace to think after the confrontation at the Burkholder farm, Nan rode Buttercup from the sunflower farm home to her *datt*'s house in town. After a much needed shower and change of clothes, she slipped into her father's small greenhouse. The revelation of Reuben's past had sent shockwaves through the gathering of locals and volunteers alike, but what troubled her most was the resignation she'd seen in his eyes—as if Dan Beachy's public accusation had confirmed something Reuben had always believed about himself.

That he was unworthy. That his mistakes defined him. That isolation was his rightful punishment.

That he didn't deserve redemption.

Inside the greenhouse, humid air enveloped her like a comforting embrace. Afternoon sunlight filtered through the glass panes, casting a gentle glow over the rows of nursery trays where her lavender cuttings grew. She moved toward them, seeking reassurance in their progress.

What she found took her breath away.

The lavender slips she'd rescued from Reuben's fields had not merely survived—they were thriving. Tiny roots extended from each cutting, reaching eagerly into the soil. New leaves had unfurled, bright green against the darker stems. It didn't take much imagination to foresee the small buds that would form soon and eventually become distinctive purple blooms.

"You're stubborn," she whispered, touching a delicate stem with her fingertip. "Just like him."

The parallel struck her with sudden clarity. These plants, damaged by fire and spared from the flood, pushed on toward life with quiet determination.

"*Gott* doesn't waste anything," her father had often told her. "Not even our mistakes."

Nan straightened, a new resolve forming within her. If these fragile cuttings could forge new roots after such devastation, surely Reuben could, too—with the right support and care.

But first, she had to stop him from leaving. Because he would leave—she had seen the decision in his eyes after Dan's cruel exposure of his past. Reuben would convince himself that disappearing was the noble choice, the protective choice, the only choice.

She wouldn't let that happen.

The crunch of tires on gravel outside drew her attention. Through the greenhouse glass, she spotted Vernon's truck pulling into the drive. The Mennonite bishop had offered to take her to the hospital in Harrisonburg to visit her father.

Nan quickly gathered her things, pausing only to sprinkle water over the lavender seedlings. "Keep growing," she urged them. "I'll be back."

Outside, Vernon greeted her with a smile that didn't quite reach his eyes. For sure he must have a great deal on his mind. "Ready to go see your *datt*?"

"*Ya*, thank you for the ride." She climbed into the passenger seat of his modest pickup truck, settling her bag at her feet. "Have you heard how he's doing today?"

"The nurse I spoke with said he's improving steadily," Vernon replied with more of his usual positivity before putting the truck in gear. "They've got him sitting up, which is a good sign with those broken ribs."

As they pulled out onto the road, Nan watched the landscape

pass by—areas of devastation interspersed with pockets that had escaped the worst of the flooding. Much like Promise itself now, she thought.

"I suspect you've got something on your mind beyond your father's health," Vernon observed after several minutes of silence.

Nan turned to study him. Vernon Mast was younger than her *datt* but bore the same air of wisdom and experience, as well as a fatherly tenderness in his eyes.

"I'm worried about Reuben," she admitted. "What Dan Beachy did yesterday—"

"Was unkind and uncalled for," Vernon finished firmly. "I doubt it would have happened if the bishop or your minister had been present. But Eli has more places to be than time to go right now, and your father..." Those reasons went without saying. "Dan will be dealt with in time."

"But maybe not in time for Reuben." Nan felt her frustrations letting loose. "Dan knew it was his chance to drive Reuben away, to make him believe he has no place among us."

Vernon nodded thoughtfully. "And you're concerned it worked."

"I know it worked," she replied. "I saw his face afterward. He's already decided to go, to spare everyone the discomfort of his presence." She bit her lip, fighting a rising tide of emotion. "As if that's what any of us want."

"Is it what you want?" Vernon asked gently.

The question hung in the air between them. Nan felt a blush warm her cheeks despite her determination to speak plainly. "I want him to stay," she said firmly. "I want him to see that one mistake—even a terrible one—doesn't define an entire life. That he has value to our community. That he..." She hesitated, then continued more softly. "That he has value to me."

Vernon's expression softened. "I thought as much." He glanced at her before returning his attention to the road. "You may be interested to know that Reuben is probably already at the hospital."

"He is?" Nan sat up straighter. "Why?"

"Visiting your father." A smile tugged at Vernon's mouth. "He left right after breakfast before you did. Hitched a ride with one of my volunteers. We have a truckload of donations waiting in Staunton, and they went to pick them up. But he also wished to pay his respects to your father and inform him of his plans to leave Promise."

Alarm shot through Nan. "Already? He's making plans so soon?"

"That was my understanding. He prefers to go with your father's blessing and recommendation to a new bishop for a new start." Vernon's calm tone did little to ease her anxiety. "Though your father may have complicated matters."

"What do you mean?"

"The bishop asked him to stay until I came this afternoon. Not sure how he convinced him to wait, but he can be persuasive."

"He is that, but maybe we need to hurry anyway." Nan couldn't keep the urgency from her voice. "Before Reuben figures out that I am coming, too."

Vernon's eyes crinkled with amusement. "I may have already increased our speed a little." He nodded toward the speedometer, which indeed showed they were traveling faster than strictly necessary. "Your father isn't the only one who sees Reuben's value."

Relief flooded through Nan. She had at least one ally in Vernon—perhaps more than one, if her father was already working to change Reuben's mind.

"Denki," she said simply.

"For the record," Vernon added, "I still hope to convince him to join one of our relief teams in North Carolina. He'd be invaluable there. And perhaps the temporary time away will make him realize what he has here in Promise. Or maybe, *who*?"

"But not if he believes he's only going to cause more harm," Nan murmured.

"Exactly." Vernon navigated a turn that brought the hospital into view on the horizon. "Sometimes a wounded man needs to be reminded that *Gott* can use broken pieces to create something new."

Nan thought of the lavender cuttings, their tiny roots reaching for nourishment, their new leaves unfurling toward the light. "Sometimes we all do."

The hospital parking lot was busier than Nan had expected. Several ambulances were parked near the entrance, while cars and trucks filled most of the available spaces. Vernon found a spot near the back and turned to Nan before shutting off the engine.

"I should mention that I didn't just offer you a ride out of kindness," he admitted. "I wanted to speak with you about Reuben."

"Oh?" Nan's curiosity piqued.

"I've known men like him before—men who carry their failures so close they can't see past them." Vernon's expression grew thoughtful. "They need someone persistent enough to keep reminding them of the truth until they finally believe it themselves."

"I'm certainly persistent," Nan replied with a small smile. "Just ask anyone in Promise."

Vernon chuckled. "But persistence alone isn't enough. It takes patience, too. And faith that what you see in him is worth fighting for, even when he can't see it himself."

The weight of his words settled over her. This wasn't just about convincing Reuben to stay or to take the position with the relief team. This was about something deeper, more permanent—about whether she was prepared to commit herself to the long, slow work of loving someone who had forgotten how to be loved.

"I understand," she said quietly.

Vernon studied her face, then nodded once, seemingly satisfied with what he found there. "Then let's go find him before he convinces himself to disappear again."

Inside the hospital, the stark white corridors and antiseptic smell reminded Nan how far they were from the familiar comforts of home. A nurse at the front desk directed them to her father's room on the second floor.

As they approached the door, Nan heard the low murmur of voices—her father's, weaker than usual but still carrying that quiet authority that had guided their church for decades, and Reuben's deeper baritone, subdued but steady.

She paused, her hand on the doorknob, suddenly uncertain. What if her presence interrupted something important? What if Reuben withdrew further at the sight of her, his walls rebuilding themselves brick by brick?

"Go on. He needs to see you," Vernon encouraged softly. "They both do."

Drawing a deep breath, Nan paused to whisper a prayer before turning the handle.

Reuben sat beside Bishop Naaman's hospital bed, hat clutched between his hands, the weight of their conversation pressing on him. He had come to pay his respects before departing Promise, a proper goodbye to the man who had welcomed him to their community five years ago. But the bishop had other ideas, drawing him into a discussion that stretched far longer than Reuben had anticipated.

"You can't run from your past forever, Reuben," the bishop was saying, his voice weaker than normal but his eyes sharp with the same wisdom that had guided the Promise community for decades. "Nor should you carry its weight alone."

"With all due respect, Bishop," Reuben replied, struggling to maintain his composure, "some burdens aren't meant to be shared. What happened in Lancaster—"

"Was five years ago," the bishop interrupted gently. "Yet you live as if it happened yesterday."

Reuben stared down at his hat, fingers tracing the brim. How could he explain that the passage of time hadn't diminished his responsibility? That the faces of those he'd harmed still visited his dreams? That Dan Beachy's public exposure had only confirmed what he'd always believed—that he had no right to a fresh start.

The sound of the door opening drew his attention. He looked up to see Nan standing in the doorway, her blue eyes widening slightly at the sight of him, and her lips turning in a pensive smile. She looked happy to see him, but cautious.

No wonder.

Vernon Mast stood just behind her, his expression unreadable. Reuben immediately rose to his feet, an instinctive gesture of respect that also served his sudden need to escape.

"Nan," the bishop greeted his daughter, reaching out a hand toward her. "*Kumm*, I've been waiting for you."

Reuben watched as she moved to her father's side, the tenderness in her greeting a reminder of all that he had denied himself for so long. The sight of her stirred emotions he'd been trying to suppress since their confrontation with Dan Beachy—longing shadowed by certainty that he had no right to what she represented.

"I should go," he said quietly, nodding to Vernon but avoiding Nan's gaze. "Let you have time with your father."

"Nay," the bishop replied with unexpected firmness. "We have not finished our discussion, Reuben Bender. And now that Nan is here, she should be part of it."

Panic flared within him. Having this conversation with the bishop alone had been difficult enough. Having it with Nan present—witnessing his shame, his weakness, his unworthiness—was more than he could bear.

"Bishop Naaman, with all due respect—" he began.

"You will show that respect by sitting down and hearing me out," the bishop interrupted, steel entering his voice despite his weakened state. "Both of you."

Reuben glanced at Vernon, hoping for some intervention, but the Mennonite bishop merely took a seat by the window, clearly intending to stay. Trapped, Reuben reluctantly lowered himself back into his chair, eyes fixed on the floor rather than risk meeting Nan's gaze.

"Now, then," the bishop began, settling against his pillows. "Reuben has just been explaining why he believes leaving Promise would be best for everyone concerned. I've been explaining why he's wrong."

Reuben's jaw tightened at this blunt summary. The bishop made it sound so simple, as if his decision was merely stubborn pride rather than the careful consideration of what was best for others—for Nan—in the long term.

"Datt," Nan began, but her father gently cut her off.

"*Nay*, let me finish," he said. "When I was trapped beneath that buggy, certain I would die there alone, I was struck by what truly matters in this life. Not our accomplishments or failures. Not even our adherence to tradition, important as that is." Reuben felt the bishop's gaze move between him and Nan. "What matters is how we love one another. How we help one another bear our burdens."

The words plucked a chord deep within him, touching beliefs he had been raised with but had somehow forgotten in the aftermath of Lancaster. Still, he couldn't surrender so easily.

"But, you must also see, too—" Reuben's hands tightened around his hat "—some burdens are not meant to be shared."

"All burdens are meant to be shared," the bishop countered with quiet certainty. "First with *Gott*, then with those

Gott places in our path for that very purpose." The older man coughed, wincing at the pain it caused his ribs, but was undeterred. "Reuben, you've carried your burden alone for too long. Is it lighter now than when you began?"

The question caught him off guard. He had never considered it that way. Looking up, he met the bishop's knowing gaze and found he couldn't lie.

"Nay," he admitted, the truth surprising even himself. "It's not."

"Because it was never yours alone to carry," the bishop said softly. "You erred in judgment, yes. The consequences were shared by many. But I dare say, those men, like Isaiah, were not compelled to follow your advice. They made their own mistakes."

Reuben shook his head, unwilling to distribute the blame he had shouldered for so long. The bishop continued undeterred.

"Even if all the wrong was yours alone, you have repented, apologized, done what you could to make things right. But the burden of restoration—that belongs to the whole community. To forgive, to rebuild, to move forward together."

A tangle of emotions knotted in Reuben's chest—doubt about the path he had chosen, longing for the acceptance being offered, a flicker of hope he immediately tried to suppress. Hope was dangerous. It led to expectations, and expectations inevitably led to disappointment.

"When Nan's sister Aubrey was sixteen," the bishop continued, his voice growing weaker, but no less determined, "she lost parts of her memory. For years, she struggled to hold on to new experiences, new knowledge. Every day was a battle."

"*Ya*, I know," Reuben replied, familiar with the story of his cousin's wife. "And now she uses that experience to help little Daniel with his struggles."

The bishop smiled at the reference to the young boy. "But she didn't fight that battle alone, just as no one expects Daniel to overcome his challenges with autism alone. Her *grossmammi* helped her develop systems to remember, to strengthen her mind. The community adjusted to her needs without judgment or impatience."

Reuben's gaze veered involuntarily to Nan, seeing her in a new light. He had known of her sister's memory issues but hadn't fully considered what that meant for the family—the patience, the adaptation, the unwavering support they had provided. The compassion he saw in Nan's face now wasn't simply kindness; it was born of experience with struggle and recovery.

"We carry each other," the bishop concluded simply. "That is our way. Our faith." He looked directly at Reuben, his gaze penetrating. "You helped save my life. Let us help restore yours."

The parallel seemed absurd. "It's not the same," he protested, though with less conviction than before.

"Isn't it?" Nan's voice startled him. She leaned forward, her blue eyes seeking his. "For years, you've hidden in your library, punishing yourself for one terrible mistake. But I've seen who you really are. During the storm, in your library, on our journey back to the farm. I've seen your strength. And I've seen how much you care."

Her words pierced the armor he had constructed around himself, touching places he thought long sealed off from the world. The way she spoke—as if she truly saw him, not just his failure or his isolation, but the man beneath it all—left him momentarily speechless.

"She's right," Vernon added from his place by the window. "You have much to offer that others desperately need. Not just in Promise, but in places that have suffered even greater devastation."

The combined weight of their arguments, their belief in him, became suddenly overwhelming. Reuben stood and paced to the window, needing physical movement to process the emotional turmoil within. Outside, the world continued its normal rhythms—hospital staff coming and going, visitors arriving, the distant mountains visible through a break in the clouds.

When he finally spoke, he couldn't keep the raw emotion from his voice. "And what happens when I fail again? When my judgment causes more harm?" The fear that had driven him for years rose to the surface. "Dan Beachy was right about one thing—my decisions cost others everything. I can't risk that again."

"You think you're protecting others by leaving," Nan observed, rising to stand before him. Her perception startled him. "But that's not the whole truth, is it? You're protecting yourself from the possibility of caring too deeply." *For me*, her eyes seemed to add, even more directly to the heart.

Her insight struck with the force of revelation. No one had ever seen through his carefully constructed reasons so completely—the deeper fears that drove him away.

"Because if you never get close to anyone," she continued softly, "you never have to risk disappointing them. Or losing them."

Something fractured within him. Her words weren't filled with indictment, but understanding, as if she, too, had felt the same need to protect herself. And there she stood, fearlessly letting down her own barriers in front of two bishops, while begging him to do the same.

For her. And for himself.

The wall he had maintained for so long, the careful distance he had kept from everyone, suddenly developed a hairline crack that threatened to spread.

He closed his eyes, overwhelmed by the truth of her words and the possibility they represented. When he opened them again, he found all three faces watching him with varying expressions of concern and hope.

"I need time," he said finally, the admission costing him dearly. "To think. To pray."

The bishop nodded, accepting this partial surrender. “That is wise. But don’t think alone, Reuben. Seek counsel. Listen to those who care for you.”

The implication that he was cared for—by the bishop, by Vernon, by Nan—sent another tremor through him. He glanced briefly at Nan, finding her watching him with an expression that made his heart quicken.

“I’ll continue to help the volunteers in Promise, for now,” he said, turning to Vernon. The words formed a commitment he hadn’t planned to make when he entered the hospital room. “And give you my decision about the North Carolina assignment, soon.”

It wasn’t a promise to stay permanently. It wasn’t even a guarantee that he would join Vernon’s relief team. But it was a step away from the certainty of departure that had driven him to the hospital that morning. A step toward possibility rather than resignation.

As the bishop leaned back against his pillows, evident satisfaction in his features despite his exhaustion, Reuben felt something shift within himself. The burden he had carried so long hadn’t lifted entirely, but for the first time in years, maybe for the first time since his *datt* had died, he might not have to carry it all alone.

He lifted his head to look at Nan. And with sudden clarity, he knew she was the one he wanted to share it with. More than anything, he wanted Nan by his side.

The thought both terrified and exhilarated him. Whatever came next, whatever decision he ultimately made, he knew he wouldn’t be making it alone.

Chapter Fifteen

Reuben arrived at the Burkholder sunflower farm just as the morning dew was beginning to burn away. He'd woken eager to see Nan. They'd gone for a walk outside of the hospital the previous day before returning to Promise.

Initially, he only wanted a short private moment with her. He hadn't intended to reveal so much of himself. But something about the way Nan had listened without judgment as they'd walked the hospital grounds had loosened the tight control he'd maintained for so long. He'd found himself telling her about Lancaster in greater detail—not just the facts Dan had exposed, but the emotions, the devastation he'd felt watching animals suffer, the sleepless nights trying to find solutions, the crushing weight of responsibility when there were none to be found.

She'd listened, really listened, in a way few ever had. And when he'd finished, she'd said something he couldn't stop turning over in his mind: "The measure of a man isn't that he never fails, but how he rises afterward."

Was it possible to rise from such a profound failure? To build something new from the ashes of the old? The bishop seemed to think so. Vernon, too. And Nan—her belief in him was so evident it almost physically hurt to acknowledge it.

He'd come to the sunflower farm early, ahead of the day's scheduled work, hoping to see her before the day became busy and chaotic.

Solomon whickered softly behind him, the mule content to crop the damp grass where he tied him to a hitching post.

"Didn't expect to find you here, again."

Reuben stiffened at the familiar voice, then turned slowly to face Dan Beachy. The other man stood at the edge of the barnyard, arms crossed over his chest, expression unreadable in the morning light.

Reuben nodded, then turned to walk to the farmhouse. He had no desire to engage further with Dan, not after the public humiliation the man had orchestrated. Whatever Dan's purpose in seeking him out this morning, Reuben doubted it was merely coincidental.

"Word is you might be joining Vernon's team in North Carolina," Dan continued, moving closer. "That would be a mistake."

And there it was—the real reason for this early morning encounter. Reuben straightened again, turning to face Dan fully.

"Why is that?" he asked, though he already knew the answer.

"Because your reputation will follow you there," Dan replied bluntly. "I've received word back from Lancaster. Isaiah and the others were…disturbed to learn of your involvement in recovery efforts."

A cold weight settled in Reuben's stomach. "I see."

"They feel you have no right to present yourself as someone qualified to help others recover from disaster." Dan's voice hardened. "Not after what you caused."

Reuben absorbed the blow silently. He had expected as much. The families who had lost their investments in his farm had every reason to resent him, to question his fitness to advise others in crisis. He couldn't blame them for that.

"I understand their concern," he said finally. "And I'll take it into consideration."

Dan stepped closer, his expression darkening. "It's not just a 'concern,' Reuben. It's a warning. Stay out of matters that could affect others' livelihoods. You've done enough damage for one lifetime."

The words echoed Reuben's own thoughts so precisely that for a moment he felt a strange kinship with the man before him—both of them believing, for different reasons, that he should remain isolated from decisions that might impact others.

But something else rose within him, too—a quiet voice that sounded remarkably like Nan's. *The measure of a man isn't that he never fails, but how he rises afterward.*

"I appreciate you delivering their message," Reuben replied evenly. "But my decision about Vernon's offer will be between me, Vernon and *Gott*."

Dan's face flushed. "You haven't changed at all, have you? Still thinking you know better than everyone else. Still willing to risk others' well-being for your own purposes."

"That's not true." The quiet assertion came from behind them, startling both men.

Nan had come around from the back entrance of the house, a basket over one arm, the morning light catching in her golden hair. Beside her, to Reuben's greater surprise, stood her grandmother, Esther Burkholder, and his cousin Jake.

"Nan," Reuben acknowledged, uncertain whether to be relieved or concerned by their arrival.

"We've been looking for you. I thought you might arrive early." Jake moved to stand beside his cousin. "Nan brought something to show you."

Dan scowled at the interruption. "This is a private conversation."

"Not anymore," *Grossmammi* Esther stated firmly, leaning on her cane as she surveyed the field. "This is Burkholder land, and we have as much right to be here as you, Dan Beachy. More, I'd say."

The elderly woman's presence seemed to take some of the wind from Dan's sails. Whatever he might say to Reuben or even to Nan, he wouldn't disrespect an elder of Esther's standing in the community.

"What do you have there, Nan?" Reuben asked, nodding toward her basket in an attempt to defuse the tension.

Nan stepped forward, setting the basket on a relatively dry patch of ground between them. "I brought these to show you," she said, drawing back a cloth to reveal several nursery trays filled with small, thriving lavender plants.

Reuben stared in disbelief. "These are—"

"From your fields," Nan confirmed. "The cuttings I took before the storm. They've rooted. They're growing." Her blue eyes held his steadily. "Even after fire and flood, they're finding a way forward."

The saplings' strong growth struck Reuben more powerfully than any argument could have. These plants—his plants—had survived through Nan's careful tending. What might have been lost forever was instead flourishing, transformed but undefeated.

Dan made a dismissive sound. "Plants aren't the same as people's livelihoods, Nan. You don't understand what's at stake here."

"I understand more than you think," she replied, turning to face him. "I understand that Reuben has spent five years punishing himself for a mistake that could have happened to anyone who tried to improve their farm."

"It wasn't just a mistake," Dan insisted. "It was arrogance. Disregard for tradition and wisdom."

"Perhaps," *Grossmammi* Esther interjected, her voice calm but carrying unexpected authority. "But I daresay he isn't alone in being guilty of youthful pride. Is there no room in our hearts for forgiveness? Do you plan to stand before *Gott* with no need for His redemption yourself, young man?"

Dan squirmed uncomfortably under her steady gaze and

likely at being reminded that she'd watched him grow from infancy. "The families in Lancaster—"

"Have forgiven him far more than you choose to acknowledge," Jake cut in. "I spoke with Isaiah myself. He readily admitted that he made his own choice to follow Reuben's lead. He wants no part in any form of retribution. When Reuben asked for his forgiveness, he gave it. He says he won't be going back on his word now. So, which tradition is more important to you, Dan? Our faithful teachings on forgiveness and turning the other cheek or traditional methods to milk your cows?"

Caught in his lies Dan sputtered, turning red-faced, and looked down.

Reuben stood very still, watching this unexpected defense unfold around him. He'd spent so long believing himself unworthy of such support that he hardly knew how to receive it now.

Dan's expression yielded, not surrender, exactly, but a grudging reassessment. "Not everyone will see it that way."

"Everyone doesn't have to." *Grossmammi* Esther dismissed Dan and moved closer to Reuben, her sharp eyes studying his face. "You came to Promise seeking a new beginning. You built a life here—quiet, perhaps too solitary, but honest and hardworking. You've honored our ways while carrying knowledge that bridges old and new." She nodded once, decisively. "Promise needs such men, especially now."

Reuben swallowed against a sudden tightness in his throat. "I don't want to cause division," he said quietly.

"You aren't causing it," Jake pointed out. "Dan's insistence on defining you by one mistake—that's what's divisive."

"I held my tongue all this time…as long as he stayed to himself." Dan's face darkened. "You can't just sweep away the consequences of his actions with pretty words about forgiveness."

"No one is suggesting that," *Grossmammi* Esther replied calmly. "Consequences remain. Trust must be rebuilt. But a man should not be exiled from acceptance forever because of one failure, no matter how grave."

Reuben knelt beside Nan's basket, gently touching one of the lavender plants with a calloused finger. Its resilience humbled him. These plants had no choice but to grow toward the light, to reach for life despite all that had befallen them. Perhaps there was wisdom in their simple persistence.

"I'm going to accept Vernon's offer," he said suddenly, rising to his feet. The decision, forming even as he spoke it, felt right in a way few things had in years. "I'll go to North Carolina with the relief team."

Jake's face split into a broad smile. "That's *goot* news, cousin."

Dan's scowl deepened. "And when they learn about Lancaster?"

"I'll tell them myself," Reuben replied steadily. "The whole truth—both my mistakes and what I've learned from them." He met Dan's gaze directly. "I can't change the past, but I can use what it taught me to help others now. I won't hide anymore. Not from what happened, and not from what I can do to help now."

Dan looked from face to face, seemingly recognizing that he'd lost this particular battle. Without another word, he turned and strode away, his stiff posture radiating disapproval.

As his figure receded, Jake clapped Reuben on the shoulder. "It's about time, cousin. Vernon will be pleased."

Grossmammi Esther nodded approvingly. "A wise choice. Now, Jake, help an old woman back to the house, would you? These fields are harder to navigate than they used to be." She glanced meaningfully between Reuben and Nan. "I think these two young people have things to discuss."

Jake's knowing smile suggested he understood perfectly. "Of course, *Grossmammi*." He offered her his arm. "Careful of that muddy patch there."

As they walked away, Reuben found himself alone with Nan

beside the basket of lavender seedlings. The morning had gone nothing like he'd expected—Dan's confrontation, the unexpected arrival of allies, his sudden decision to join Vernon's team. But most surprising of all was the lightness he felt.

"How did you know?" he asked Nan quietly. "It's like the three of you were just waiting to pounce on Dan Beachy."

Nan's smile held a touch of her usual mischief. "I pay attention," she replied simply.

"Ya." A lightheartedness flooded over him, and he laughed. "I know you do."

Nan couldn't remember anything that had made her so happy of late as it did to hear Reuben laugh. A real true laugh—something she thought he must have forgotten how to do.

She watched as Jake led her *grossmammi* back toward the farmhouse, their departure as deliberate as their arrival had been. Her grandmother's meddling was as transparent as spring water, but Nan couldn't find it in her heart to be anything but grateful. Especially after witnessing Reuben stand his ground against Dan Beachy.

"We'll see you both for breakfast," Jake called over his shoulder, not even attempting to disguise the knowing smile that spread across his face.

When they were finally all alone, Nan turned her attention back to the basket of lavender seedlings between them. She knelt to adjust the cloth covering, suddenly aware of a flutter of nervousness in her stomach.

She looked up, unable to suppress the smile that rose to her lips. "I wish you could have heard *Grossmammi* as we walked out here. She said she'd 'had enough of that man's self-righteousness to last a lifetime.'"

"Your grandmother is a formidable woman," he said.

"She is," Nan agreed, smoothing the cloth back over her precious plants. The tiny sprouts had grown stronger with each passing day, their resilience a constant reminder of possibility after devastation. "*Grossmammi* also pointed out something interesting about you."

She hadn't planned to share this, but something about the moment—the quiet understanding between them, the absence of the walls Reuben usually maintained—gave her courage.

"Oh?" Reuben raised an eyebrow, curiosity mingled with wariness in his expression.

Nan drew a deep breath. "She said you remind her of my grandfather—quieter than most, but with depths others don't always see." She met his gaze directly, determined not to shy away from the truth as she continued. "She said he used to worry too much about making mistakes, too. Until he learned that most mistakes can be mended, with time and care and help from those who love you."

The word *love* hung in the air between them, and Nan felt heat rise to her cheeks. She hadn't meant to be so forward, yet she couldn't bring herself to regret the implication. Not when Reuben was looking at her with such tender bewilderment, as if she was a puzzle he'd given up hoping to solve.

"North Carolina is far," he said after a moment, his voice lower than before. "Vernon says the work could take months."

"Ya," she acknowledged, trying to ignore the pang in her heart at the thought of such a long separation. "It could."

"I'd be away from Promise. From..." He hesitated, seeming to search for the right words.

The unfinished sentence hung between them, heavy with meaning. Nan summoned her courage once more. "From me?"

He nodded, his gaze searching her face with an intensity that might once have made her uncomfortable. Now, it simply made her certain.

"Distance isn't always a bad thing," she said carefully, choosing her words with deliberate precision. "It gives clarity sometimes. Perspective. Remember, you told me that." She rose to her feet, brushing traces of soil from her apron. "And letters can bridge many miles."

"Letters," Reuben repeated, and the slow smile that spread across his face sent a wave of warmth through her. "You would write to me?"

"Ya," she replied simply, her heart beating faster at his evident pleasure in the idea. "If you would welcome it."

The change in his expression was subtle but profound—a lightening around his eyes, a softening at the corners of his mouth, as if a burden he'd carried for so long was finally beginning to ease. "I would like that very much."

Joy bubbled up within her, and she couldn't help but return his smile with one of her own. "Then it's settled." She gestured toward the basket of lavender plants. "And when you return, these will be ready to transplant. A new beginning for your fields."

"*Our* fields," he corrected, then froze, appearing startled by his own words.

The implication stole Nan's breath. *Our fields*. Two simple words that suggested a future she had scarcely dared to imagine—one where their lives were intertwined, where what belonged to him also belonged to her. Where they worked side by side not just in crisis or recovery, but in the everyday business of living.

She felt her eyes widen, but she didn't retreat from the suggestion. Instead, she nodded slowly, allowing the possibility to take root in her heart. "I would like that," she said softly. "To see them bloom again. Together."

Looking into Reuben's eyes, she saw a reflection of her own tender new hope—a willingness to explore what might grow between them, given time and care and patience.

"Together," he agreed, and the word carried the weight of a vow. "Nan, there's something else I'd very much like before I must go."

"What's that?" She looked up into his earnest golden eyes, so deep and full of affection her knees weakened.

"To thank you for believing in me." He took her free hand gently in his own, then lifted it to his lips and placed a tender kiss across her knuckles.

Heart pounding, she captured his fingers in hers and lifted the palm of her hand, tenderly cupping his cheek. "And thank you, Reuben Bender, for seeing me for who I am."

He dipped his head and touched his lips to hers with a kiss that was over far too fast. "Soon, Nan…soon we will be together." His voice held powerful conviction. "And nothing will keep me apart from you again."

As they gathered up the basket of lavender seedlings and started back toward the farmhouse, Nan felt a certainty settling within her, as solid and reassuring as the earth beneath her feet. Whatever challenges lay ahead—Reuben's months in North Carolina, the ongoing recovery in Promise, the slow process of helping him fully integrate into the community—they would face them not as separate individuals, but as partners in a shared journey.

She glanced sideways at him as they walked, noting how his stride had unconsciously shortened to match hers, how the morning light caught in his beard and brought out auburn highlights she'd never noticed before. His profile against the brightening sky seemed different somehow—still strong, still serious, but no longer weighed down by resignation.

Nan's imagination had always been full, and yet she'd scarcely dared to dream the happiness she felt now could be hers. But now, carrying these tender plants that had survived against all odds, walking beside a man who was finding his way back from years of self-imposed exile, she allowed herself to dream after all.

Of lavender fields blooming purple beneath summer skies.

Of letters exchanged over winter months, bridging the distance with words.

Of a homecoming in spring, when both plants and people might put down new roots.

Of a future where *together* was not just a word but a way of life.

As they reached the farmhouse, where breakfast and family and the day's work awaited, Nan held these dreams close, like seeds planted in fertile soil. With time and care, they would grow. Of that, she was certain.

And if there was one thing Nan Burkholder had in abundance, it was patience for things worth growing.

Epilogue

Nan stood at the edge of the lavender field, a warm July breeze carrying the fresh scent of their flowers. The plants she had rescued and nurtured through the winter were now thriving in neat rows across the eastern section of what was now *their*—Nan and Reuben Bender's—farm. Farther down, freshly tilled earth held thousands of new small shrubs that would mature into a full field by next year.

Just eight weeks since their wedding, and already the land was transforming, much like their lives had transformed over the past year.

She smiled as she heard the familiar sound of Reuben's footsteps approaching from behind. His tread was different now—lighter, less burdened than when she'd first come seeking lavender cuttings from his fields after the fire.

"They're looking strong," he said, coming to stand beside her. His work-worn hand found hers, their fingers intertwining with the easy familiarity that still sometimes surprised her.

"Ya," she agreed, leaning slightly against his solid presence. "The ones I kept in the greenhouse have established well." She gestured toward the newer plantings. "And next year, if *Gott* wills it, we'll have a full crop."

Reuben nodded, his amber eyes surveying their growing fields with quiet satisfaction. "I never thought I'd see them bloom again," he admitted softly.

"I did," Nan replied, squeezing his hand. "From the moment I took those first cuttings."

He turned to look at her, a smile crinkling the corners of his eyes. "You've always seen possibilities others miss."

"Including you?" she teased gently.

"Especially me." He brought their joined hands to his lips, pressing a kiss against her knuckles—a gesture that still sent warmth coursing through her.

The sound of buggy wheels and voices drifted toward them from the direction of the farmhouse. Nan glanced at her watch, the practical timepiece a wedding gift from her father.

"That must be *Datt* and the others," she said. "Right on time."

Reuben nodded, reluctantly releasing her hand. "I should make sure everything is ready at the library."

"It's been ready since yesterday," Nan reminded him with a fond smile. "You've already checked it twice."

A hint of his old uncertainty flickered across his face, then dissolved into rueful acknowledgment. "I want it to be perfect. This is important."

"It will be perfect," she assured him. "But not because every book is precisely aligned or because you've dusted the shelves three times. It will be perfect because you're sharing something precious with people who matter to you."

The tension in his shoulders eased. "When did you become so wise?"

"I married a very thoughtful man," she replied, her smile widening. "He's been a good influence."

Together they walked back toward the house, passing through rows of lavender and along a newly graveled path that connected their modest home with the stone library in the woods. Reuben had built the path after his return from North Carolina, making the once secret sanctuary accessible to visitors—an intentional decision to remain connected with their community.

As they rounded the final curve in the path, the library came into view, its stone chimney and timber walls standing strong and welcoming in the spring sunshine. Outside, buggies were already gathered, their horses tied to a hitching post Reuben had installed just for such occasions.

"Nan! Reuben!" Tommy's excited voice carried across the clearing as the boy spotted them. He'd grown taller during the months his uncle had been away with the relief team. Beside him, Daniel bounced with barely contained excitement.

"Can we show *Dawdi* Naaman that book?" Daniel asked, rushing toward them. "The one with bears!"

"Of course," Reuben replied, ruffling the boy's hair affectionately. "That's why we're opening the library today—so everyone can enjoy the books."

Nan's heart swelled as she watched Reuben with the boys. His months in North Carolina had transformed him in ways she wouldn't have imagined. Working alongside others to rebuild flood-ravaged communities, he had finally begun to see himself as a helper rather than a source of harm. The letters they'd exchanged—sometimes arriving in bundles when poor roads delayed deliveries—had allowed them to know each other's hearts in a way that might not have happened otherwise.

By the time he returned to Promise in February, both Reuben and Nan were ready to plan their life together. Their wedding in May had been a celebration not just of their love, but of restoration—of trust rebuilt, of new beginnings, of faith rewarded.

"There you are," her *datt* greeted them as they approached the gathering. Despite the cane he still used, the bishop had recovered enough to manage his farrier business with help from Lukas, who remained in Promise to help him. His eyes twinkled as he added, "The newlyweds finally emerge from their fields."

"Datt," Nan laughed, embracing him. "We were just checking the new plantings."

Aubrey and Jake joined them, little Sophie cradled in Aubrey's arms—the newest addition to their family, born just two weeks ago. *Grossmammi* Esther sat on a bench nearby, holding court with several of the elders who had come for the library's official opening.

"Shall we begin?" Reuben asked, his voice steady, though Nan could detect the slight nervousness beneath. Sharing his sanctuary was a deliberate choice, yet still a somewhat frightening one for him.

At her father's nod, Reuben led the way to the library entrance. The massive wooden door, once locked against visitors, stood wide open in welcome. He paused at the threshold, gathering his thoughts, and Nan moved to stand supportively at his side.

"For many years," he began, his deep voice carrying easily to the small gathering, "this place was my refuge from the world. A place to hide away with books and memories." His gaze swept over the faces watching him—neighbors, church members, friends and family. "But I've learned that knowledge kept to oneself serves little purpose. These books—histories of our region, farming texts, weather records kept by my grandfather and father—they belong to us all now."

The bishop stepped forward, leaning on his cane. "We are grateful, Reuben. Especially for the children, who will learn from these resources in ways that honor both our traditions and the wisdom *Gott* has provided through the study of His creation."

As if on cue, the schoolteacher, Sarah Yoder, brought forward several of her students. "The children have prepared something to share their thanks," she said with a gentle smile.

The small group of students, ranging from six to fourteen years old, recited a poem they had memorized about the importance of learning. Nan watched Reuben's face as he listened, seeing the emotion he tried to contain behind his calm exterior.

When the children finished, everyone moved inside to explore the library. Reuben had arranged the space thoughtfully, creating a special section of appropriate books for the school children, areas dedicated to agriculture and weather, and comfortable seating for reading and study.

As the once solitary space filled with conversation, Nan noticed a truck pulling up to the edge of the clearing. She touched Reuben's arm, directing his attention to the unexpected arrival.

"Is that—" he began, surprise evident in his voice.

"The Elliotts," Nan confirmed as James, Sarah, Michael and Emma emerged from the vehicle.

Reuben excused himself and moved quickly toward the English family they'd sheltered during the flood. Nan followed, her heart warming at the genuine pleasure on Reuben's face.

"We didn't expect you," he said, shaking James's hand firmly before being enveloped in a surprising hug from the man.

"We couldn't make it for your wedding," Sarah explained, embracing Nan warmly. "But when James got a break from his job, we knew we had to come see you both—and this place that sheltered us during the storm."

Emma, who appeared to have grown several inches since they'd last seen her, looked around with wide eyes. "It looks so different without all the rain and mud!"

"It is different," Nan agreed, smiling at the girl. "Just like we're all a little different after what we went through together."

Michael nodded thoughtfully. "Dad says what happened here changed all our lives. Made us appreciate what matters."

"Your father is a wise man," Reuben said. "Come inside—we're sharing the library with our community today. You're part of that story, too."

As the Elliotts joined the gathering inside, Nan stood for a moment in the doorway, taking in the scene before her. The library hummed with life—children exploring books under Sarah's guidance, farmers discussing weather journals with Reuben, her sisters and *Grossmammi* examining the stained glass window.

The past years' journey unfolded in her mind—from the fire that had devastated Reuben's fields, to the flood that had nearly claimed her father, to the revelation of Reuben's past that had threatened to drive him away. Each crisis had seemed like an ending, yet each had ultimately opened a door to something new—recovery, forgiveness, love.

"Penny for your thoughts?" Reuben's voice brought her back to the present as he rejoined her in the doorway.

"I was thinking about how we came to this special moment," she replied, leaning against him as his arm slipped around her waist. "How places change. How people change. How what once seemed broken beyond repair can bloom again."

He nodded, his gaze moving from the lively gathering inside to the lavender fields visible in the distance. "Like our fields."

"Like our hearts," she corrected gently, facing him fully.

His amber eyes, once so guarded, now looked at her with open adoration. "I never thought I'd have this again," he admitted quietly. "A home that's truly home. Work that matters. People who see past my mistakes." His hand came up to cup her cheek. "You, most of all. My greatest blessing."

"We bless each other," Nan replied, covering his hand with her own. "That's what *Gott* intended, I think. Not perfection, but growth. Not isolation, but love."

"Ich liebe dich," he murmured, the Pennsylvania Dutch phrase for "I love you" seeming to come more easily to him in their mother tongue. "More than I can say."

Behind them, the library buzzed with joyful conversation. Beyond them, the lavender fields stretched toward the horizon, their purple blooms symbolic of restoration, both physical and spiritual. And between them, in the quiet space where their hearts met, the future unfolded like a promise—tender, resilient and endlessly renewed.

Like the lavender, they had survived fire and flood. Like the library, they had opened to new possibilities. And like the love growing between them, they would continue to transform—season by season, challenge by challenge, joy by joy—blooming again and again in the fertile soil of faith, forgiveness and abiding love.

* * * * *

Dear Reader,

Thank you for joining me on this return to my beloved Blue Ridge Mountains and the fictional Amish community of Promise, Virginia. Don't you think this setting begs for fairy-tale stories? I certainly do, and so Bishop Naaman's daughters shall have them. I hope you enjoyed the Beauty and the Beast and redemption themes in Nan and Reuben's story. It was my absolute delight and privilege to bring them together while also paying homage to the resilience of Appalachia through the devastating floods from Hurricane Helene.

And the good news is that the fairy-tale romances in Promise continue. Watch for Rose and Lukas's Red Riding Hood–inspired romance coming in fall 2026.

Until next time,
Amy Grochowski